A punch of icy air hit her square in the back.

Only sheer willpower kept her from bolting. That, and pride.

Only when she'd gained control, did she turn and confront the man she'd once loved.

"Hello, Lachesis." Eyes—the color of pewter and just as cold—caught hers, their interest unflinching. "Did you really expect a locked door would keep me out?"

Lachesis? So it was going to be like that.

What *had* she expected, a vow of undying love?

"No, *Prometheus*." Celeste's gaze swept over Cain's off-white jeans and equally light trenchcoat. "I had expected you to drop dead, but life is full of little disappointments, isn't it?"

It had been almost three years since she'd seen him, but in one glance she realized that he hadn't changed.

Not physically, anyway.

DONNA YOUNG

ENGAGING BODYGUARD

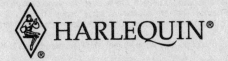

HARLEQUIN®

TORONTO • NEW YORK • LONDON
AMSTERDAM • PARIS • SYDNEY • HAMBURG
STOCKHOLM • ATHENS • TOKYO • MILAN • MADRID
PRAGUE • WARSAW • BUDAPEST • AUCKLAND

To Kate Stevenson, Rhonda Kramer
and Shannon Godwin.
For your guidance, your faith and your infinite patience.
Thank you.

ISBN 0-373-22908-9

ENGAGING BODYGUARD

Copyright © 2006 by Donna Young

This edition published by arrangement with Harlequin Books S.A.

® and TM are trademarks of the publisher. Trademarks indicated with
® are registered in the United States Patent and Trademark Office, the
Canadian Trade Marks Office and in other countries.

www.eHarlequin.com

Printed in U.S.A.

ABOUT THE AUTHOR

Donna Young, an incurable romantic, lives in beautiful Northern California with her husband and two children.

Books by Donna Young

HARLEQUIN INTRIGUE
824—BODYGUARD RESCUE
908—ENGAGING BODYGUARD

CAST OF CHARACTERS

Celeste Pavenic—The government's number one profiler until the president's son is murdered. Now she's their number one suspect.

Cain MacAlister—As a government operative, Cain vows to find the truth behind the murder of the president's son. But when a high-ranking official becomes the next target, will the truth force him to choose between the woman he loves and his duty to his country?

Gabriel—An elusive assassin with a deadly agenda—one that throws Celeste and Cain into a desperate race against the clock.

Ian MacAlister—Cain's younger brother and an ex-Navy SEAL with a reputation for getting the job done—whatever it takes.

Quamar Bazan—Cain's friend and a black ops agent whose faith in Allah equals his trust in a quiet step and a sharp blade.

Chapter One

The sky was a flat black, the air dense with the promise of snow. Distant laughter sliced through the cold; on its heels came a spattering of cheers and clinking crystal.

Cain MacAlister tossed off a double shot of hundred-year-old Scotch, embracing the bite on his tongue, the burn when it hit his gut.

He didn't believe in happily ever after.

Hell, he didn't believe in happily ever anything.

Cain settled into the terrace shadows, enjoying the darkness that stretched around him. He poured himself another drink—three fingers high this time—from the bottle he'd grabbed from the bar.

His mother had certainly outdone herself with the reception. Politicians, celebrities and the world's wealthiest packed the ballroom in honor of his sister Kate's wedding. He'd even noted a royal or two. None, however, outshone the newlyweds he'd left twirling around the dance floor, laughing and hugging, oblivious to those watching.

Mr. and Mrs. Roman D'Amato.

The wind—driven upward from the Manhattan streets—snatched at Cain's shirt collar, its icy fingers flexing in the night air.

Unhurried, Cain leaned back against the wall, welcoming the chill from the cement when it penetrated the thin layer of his tuxedo. As the days approached the end of March, the weather tended to hang on to the colder temperatures of the Atlantic. But the bitter cold, the razor-sharp cuts of the wind, simply assured his solitude.

He set the liquor bottle onto a nearby ledge just as a muffled *thwump* hit the air. *Careful,* a warning whispered—its hum vibrating through his Celtic blood. Cain straightened, his stance predatory.

A clump of snow falling?

Maybe.

His hand slid over the Glock nestled in his shoulder holster, only to stop mid motion, the polymer cool beneath his fingertips. Hearing nothing, he shifted forward until he detected the faint scent of cigar smoke. Heavily spiced, unmistakably Cuban.

With a grunt, Cain let his hand drop from the pistol. "Joining me for a celebratory drink, Jon?"

"No." Jonathon Mercer, the director of Labyrinth—an elite branch of the CIA—stepped from the darkness into the fringe light of the ballroom's French doors. In spite of his sixty-odd years, Jon was a strong, broad-shouldered man with a shock of white hair and features so sharp, he looked as if he'd been hewn from granite.

With a jab of his cigar, he pointed toward Cain's glass. "Isn't that a bit much, even for you?"

"Not tonight." Cain had been weaned on Scotch.

Both men knew it would take more than a few shots to put him under the table.

"It won't bring Diana Taylor back," the old man bit out, his tone surly enough to spark an argument.

Cain brought the tumbler to his lips. "You're right." In one gulp, he drained the glass, using the alcohol to blur the memories of long hair the color of polished mahogany, the laser-blue eyes that were quick to flash with intelligence and, when spurred, passion.

"Damn it, Cain. It's been three years. Diana's murder was unavoidable. No one could've anticipated that car bomb."

"Let it go, Jon." Diana had been petite, delicate in nature as well as build. She'd deserved a better...what? Cain caught himself. Death? Life? A better fiancé? An ache pulled somewhere under his heart, but this time he didn't pour another drink. Tonight, even the bite of whiskey couldn't fill the emptiness.

"Not until you let *her* go." When Cain didn't answer, Mercer tried again. "Look, I might have been only her boss, but I cared for her, too," he said, his tone edged with irritation over the admission. "Not only was she the best damned profiler we had, but she was a hell of a woman."

"Your point?"

"Labyrinth is Black Ops. You've worked for me long enough to know the game. Hell, in the last ten years, you rewrote the damn play book." Mercer took a short puff on his cigar. After a moment, he glanced over the balcony to the hazy glow of the city street seventy floors below. "She understood the risks of the job, Prometheus," he murmured, his voice rough, sandpaper against sandpaper. "We all do."

"Do we?" Cain ignored the use of his code name and set his glass on the ledge by the bottle. Living with the grief had become easy, but the emptiness? He'd found that words, no matter how sympathetic, couldn't fill the void that entombed him.

"What if she *had* lived? What then?"

"We'll never know will we?" But Cain knew. "And what about Diana's grandmother? Did she deserve to die with Diana?"

"There are always casualties."

"And if it had been Lara, Jon? What if it had been your daughter burning to death?"

Mercer's blue eyes became twin shards of ice, but the man didn't answer. Cain suspected he couldn't. "Forget it." Cain said, even though he knew they both wouldn't. Ever. "You didn't come out here to play counselor. What do you want?"

Mercer sighed, admitting defeat. "Peace and quiet." He leaned his hip against the balcony railing and unbuttoned his coat. The wind caught at the front tails, slamming them against the cement until metal jingled. Frowning, Mercer patted his jacket, then reached in the pocket. "This was the closest I could come to both."

"Lucky me."

"I thought so." Mercer's hand froze. "What the hell?" He pulled out a small, white envelope and ripped it open. Several coins spilled into his palm. "Damn it!"

"Quarters?" Cain asked as another warning whispered from the far recesses of his mind. In the space of one heartbeat, Cain palmed his gun.

But he was too late. Two muffled pops hit the air, so close together each sound almost blended into one. Mercer jerked, then took a step back trying to recover. His features slanted with shock.

Cain grabbed for Mercer, his fingertips snagging the older man by his tuxedo lapels preventing him from tumbling.

"Jon." Deftly, he lowered Mercer onto the mosaic tile, using the cement railing for cover. Cursing, Cain unbuttoned Mercer's coat. The air between them clogged with the metallic scent of blood. Gut-shot. Two perfectly placed holes—an inch apart—tattooed his stomach. "Stay with me, Jon."

For a brief second, Cain tilted his head, obtaining a clear view of the highrises, stories of glass and steel, flanking their hotel. The shot could've come from any one of a hundred different places. Although unlikely, the possibility remained that whoever had taken Mercer down was out there, still observing.

Mercer drew a shallow breath. "The coins...a warning." The words were barely audible, forcing Cain to place an ear by his friend's mouth. "Find Diana."

"Diana?" Disbelief ripped through Cain, tearing his heart wide open. He grabbed Jon, fisting the lapel this time. "Diana's dead," he demanded in a harsh whisper.

"No." Mercer shoved the coins into Cain's hand— warm, sticky blood now coating the metal. "Hiding."

Mercer's eyes fluttered shut. "Shadow Point. Do...it." The coins dug into Cain's palm, his jaw tightened.

Diana alive? His mind raced, calculating the possibilities, searching for reasons.

Finding none, the betrayal settled deep, merging with rage, filling the void.

If Diana *was* alive, he'd find her.

Then after?

She'd better run like hell.

Chapter Two

The asphalt path—wet and salt-ridden—dulled the rhythmic slap of Celeste Pavenic's running shoes. She tried, unsuccessfully, to concentrate on the sound and ignore the fatigue burning behind her eyelids, leaving them gritty and sore.

In the distance, Lake Huron bellowed. Its ice-ridden waves hammered the rocks, agitated by the strength of the northeasterly wind.

Feeling the same restlessness, she doubled her pace. Her muscles screamed in protest, her lungs dragged in the frost-bitten air, but she only pushed harder. Under her sweatshirt, Lycra clung to her damp skin—and to her gun, its holster snug against the small of her back.

God, she hated running.

Dodging patches of ice, Celeste veered past a rusted pipe gate, where a No Trespassing sign banged an unsteady rhythm in the wind.

She turned onto the lighthouse's gravel road, more snow than pebbles, and navigated the steep incline that spilled out to the keeper's cottage—now a small museum for the summer tourists.

Several yards beyond, the lighthouse's lone, white-washed column of stone appeared stark and haggard against the craggy rocks of the point. A few windows dotted its walls, all framed with emerald-green shutters, vivid enough in the dimming light to soften the harshness.

She circled around the side of the tower, stopping only when she reached its weatherbeaten door. With one last step, she collapsed against the pine then gracelessly slid to the ground.

On her knees, she sucked in long, deep jags of oxygen and waited for the blood to cease pounding through her temples. Overhead, the seagulls cried, their evening rant somehow soothing now that she'd finished.

Every day, for the past three years, she'd forced herself to run five miles. Never the same route, never the same time, but always five miles.

And twice a month she rewarded herself with a visit inside the lighthouse. With a slight shift of her head, she took in her surroundings. Pleased that she was alone, she slipped a piece of strong but flexible plastic from her sock and shoved it into the lock. Once placed in contact with the metal, Celeste counted to ten while it expanded, shaped then hardened into a key.

After having lost her other key earlier in the month, Celeste grinned over the fact that once again she had access to the tower, access that was usually limited to the county's historical society.

With one twist, the shoved open the door.

After another quick check, Celeste entered, then shut it behind her and ran up the hundred-odd feet of iron spiral stairs.

Solace. That was her reward, if only for a brief moment in time. She stepped through the steel trapdoor of the lens room and outside onto the iron walkway.

Waves rushed in, crashing against the rocks, then retreating in leisure—one piling on top of another, making it difficult for the gulls as they dipped and skated over the water, searching for their dinner.

Celeste leaned forward, her palms spread on the railing. Thin shafts of daylight pierced the curtains of clouds that hung low over the slash of gray lake. She angled her face into the sun's rays, attempting to absorb some of its warmth, chase away the evening chill that had already seeped her bones. This was her time, her moment of peace when she shut out the world. She breathed in the heavy scent of pine and decaying sand reeds, tasted the moisture—letting the familiarity untwist the knots deep within her belly.

"So it's true."

Celeste swung around, her feet braced, her fists high ready to swing.

Eyes the color of pewter and just as cold caught hers, stopping her heart, stopping her dead.

"Cain."

He stood only a few steps away, his shoulder resting against the door's trim, the lean lines of his face set as firm as the stone behind him.

"Hello, Diana."

The name sounded foreign, it had been that long. Her fists dropped to her side, but they didn't unclench.

"It's Celeste," she corrected. Wary, her gaze drifted over his worn jeans, black shirt and black leather jacket, noting the violence that rode the unyielding lines beneath. "Diana died a long time ago."

"Celeste," Cain drawled, testing, his tone a rough wool that slid over her, its texture abrasive with anger.

The anger should have frightened her. But these last years had been too desolate. Her dreams too vivid.

"Pavenic, right?"

His eyebrow rose when his gaze rested on her hair. Automatically, her fingers touched the short, feathered ends, now sweat-dampened and plastered to her forehead. In the past, her hair had lain in long, easy waves past her shoulders. It had been Diana's one vanity—and to Celeste a potentially deadly encumbrance.

"That's quite a name."

"It's more than a name, Cain. It's who I am." His hair, she noticed, was the same thick mane of black pitch. Once professionally tapered—it now hung in disarray, roughened by the wind. Not long enough to be shabby, but wild and untamed enough to tempt a woman's fingers to dive deep, to feel its soft tickle against her palm.

When her own palm did just that, Celeste's throat went dry. She wanted to look away, but it had been so long. Greedily, she drank in the lean muscle, long bones and breadth of shoulder in one slow pull. He was a man who commanded attention, and sometimes with it, respect—but more often, caution.

Her gaze drifted to the dark ends of hair curled

around the collar of his jacket. They added a savage edge to the aristocratic slant of his cheekbones, making them seem stronger, unbending—defining the confidence beneath. The kind of confidence that came with rigid beliefs, heritage and years of discipline.

A warrior.

And at one time, she thought, her warrior.

"How did you find…" her voice trailed off. Emotions swirled in her. Fear, anger, confusion were only the few she could identify. Through it all, she realized only Jonathon Mercer could've sent Cain. And for only one reason. "Jonathon?"

"Dead." The word was clipped, business-dry—not surprising considering Cain had delivered it.

Duty first.

She'd known, of course. A split second before she saw the shadows flicker in the iron-gray of Cain's eyes. Still, the grief sliced through her, razor-sharp. She wanted to double over, rock back and forth to keep the pain at bay, but knew from experience neither would help. Death was final. Nothing changed that.

"How?" she asked, her fists now clenched for a different reason. "Who?"

"Murdered. Double tap to the stomach."

She waited, wanting more. When he didn't offer, her fists rose to hip level, her knuckles turned white. "The details, Cain. Give them to me."

"You mean, other than the fact that you're in hiding? That you might be in danger?" He lifted a negligent shoulder. "I have none. Jonathon died too quickly."

Her muscles loosened, but only slightly. Celeste

believed him. If Jonathon had been forewarned, he would've contacted her. "I don't suppose if I tell you to go, you'll do it?"

"Not until I get some answers."

He deserved them, she knew. And much more. She'd taken part of his life from him—for the right reasons—and left him grief in its place. No one had that right, but she'd taken it anyway. Just as she'd do again, if it meant keeping him safe.

"I half expected plastic surgery."

Startled, Celeste frowned. "Your mother would've made it…difficult." Cain's mother, Christel MacAlister, specialized in reconstructive surgery, mostly with children born with deformities. But as an expert in her field, she ranked among the top in the world. Celeste hadn't wanted to risk the possibility she'd find out. "Even with thousands of plastic surgeons in the world, I still didn't want to risk the possibility that Christel—"

"I suggest…" He hadn't raised his voice, but the icy tone sent shivers down her spine. "…we don't discuss my family right now."

"The intention was never to hurt—" She caught herself, tried to loosen the guilt that seized her chest. "Besides, Shadow Point is far enough off the beaten track, surgery didn't seem necessary."

"How far off the beaten track can you be when Olivia Cambridge lives down the road?" His laugh was harsh, steel scraping stone. "Having the president's mother within a few miles must bring a tourist or two."

"Some. More soon," she admitted, suddenly unsteady with doubt. Angry that she'd been with him only a few moments and the inadequacy had returned, clutching her gut. "When the Cambridge Auction begins. I've been here since...for quite a while and never had a problem."

"Olivia Cambridge doesn't know who you are then." It was a statement more than a question, but she chose to answer it anyway.

"You mean, she doesn't know that I was the lead suspect in her grandson's murder?" She shifted, unable to ease through the pang of regret. "Yes, she knows."

"And President Cambridge?" Cain straightened and studied her, his eyes flashing like finely brushed silver. "Does he realize you're living in his home town?"

Celeste was first to blink and hated herself for it.

"No," she bit out, her jaw hurting with the effort. "It's complicated. Too complicated for me to explain."

"Complications I can handle. Lies..." He paused. "Not so much."

"The lies go with the job. Your job. And I haven't asked you to handle anything. Not in a long time." When his gaze caught hers this time, the arrogance flashed, then disappeared—but not before it ignited her temper. "I'm not going to start now. Go home, Cain. I don't want you here." When she tried to walk past, he snagged her arm. Little shots of electricity, sparked. His fingers flexed as if he'd felt the sting too.

"Jon's dead. What you want or don't want doesn't concern me." Oh, his stance was deceptively casual and emphasized the force of his chest and the leanness of his hips. But she was no fool. Not anymore.

She shook him off, then stepped forward, a scorching storm of anger driving her until they were almost toe to toe.

"God, you haven't changed have you?" Celeste asked rhetorically.

He was taller than most, certainly much taller than her. Just shy of a foot, she remembered. But it took more than height to intimidate her. "I did what was necessary."

Surprise caught his features, if only for a millisecond. If she hadn't been watching she'd have missed it. Diana had never taken a stand against him.

Good, she thought, better for him to know now she'd changed.

"Necessary for who?" Cain prodded.

"For everyone." Faking her death might have been drastic, but she still believed the reasons held fast.

She had to. Or she'd have gone insane.

"Does that include Grace, too? Or do you have her hidden somewhere?"

The insult plunged deep at the mention of her grandmother, a mortal wound, as had been intended. Her composure slipped, but her stance didn't. "She died in the explosion."

"Yet you survived."

She hadn't wanted to. The high-pitched screams of terror. Her grandmother's hands clawing the window, the sweet sickening scent of burning flesh mingling with the more rancid odor of burning hair.

Fixing a sneer on her face, she pushed away the nightmare. She'd changed her identity in order to find Grams' killer. Walked away from her past. Except for the ring, she admitted, feeling the metal warm and comforting against her skin, its sapphire hidden between her breasts.

Both the ring and the name Pavenic—a surname of Romanian gypsies—had given Celeste courage. And with it, a new life.

"Survival is a matter of perspective," she answered, her words clipped, her control back in place. "You wouldn't understand, Cain."

"That's where you're wrong, *Celeste*," his voice dropped, his smile glacial enough to freeze her blood. Without warning, he grabbed her shoulders and hauled her to him. "The last several years provided me with an enormous amount of perspective."

"WELL, WELL, what do we have here?" The man's question slid through tightened teeth, its vicious edge lost in the shrill whistle of the wind.

He shifted his position, leaning farther back against the boulder, leaving him a line of sight through the crowded pines. His thumb moved over the dial until the high-powered scope brought both Prometheus and the woman into view. Satisfaction rolled through him. The fact that Prometheus had appeared in Shadow Point so soon hadn't surprised him. When an outcome is planned, there is little to be surprised over.

He studied the woman, noting the way she stood, her back straight, her features defiant—enough to make his finger tighten on the rifle's trigger. The cold metal urged him to apply more pressure, but he controlled the impulse with little effort.

A bullet maimed, even killed. Both ways brought pain.

But not the excruciating pain she would soon endure.

Not for the money. Or his reputation.

Merely because of the pleasure.

For three months, he'd known she'd die. And during that time, he'd savored the taste of her death as he would have a fine merlot. His lips twisted, their slant feral. A soft, subtly sweet—blood-red—Merlot.

For now, he'd watch, indulge his curiosity. If she and Prometheus hadn't joined forces over Mercer's demise, they soon would. Incentive—if the correct incentive— tempted even the most cautious. And the coins…well, that was just pure genius.

He considered the possibilities. His plans weren't so set that he couldn't adjust them a bit. For the time being, he'd increase the stakes just a little. After all, he had a point to make.

Lachesis…Prometheus…

Even together, they were no match for him.

"LET ME GO." Blue eyes, now diamond-hard, met Cain's unflinchingly. The movement turned her features into the dimming sunlight. Except for the stubborn chin, her face was a perfect oval, framed by short, disheveled wisps of honey-colored hair.

Familiar enough to feed his rage. Feminine enough to make him resent it.

"I don't have the answers you're looking for," she insisted. "And if I did, why believe anything I'd say?" She glanced away for just a moment. Enough to tell him that dealing with the truth of that statement was still a struggle for her. "I killed the president's son."

"It was never proven."

"That's just semantics. Alive or dead, we both know I'll never be truly free from suspicion." Her tone remained cool and unattached, with no trace of self-pity. "So why trust me?"

"Oh, I don't trust you, sweetheart," he said, knowing his grip must be hurting her. But he refused to care. Refused to give in to anything but the rage. "Not any farther than I could bury you." He brought her closer until her gasp warmed his cheek, leaving no room for the wind to weaken the floral scent that clung to her hair. But it wasn't enough. Not for the past years of hell. God, he'd almost wanted her to be maimed, scarred, half dead—anything to show she'd reason not to contact him. But instead, he'd found her running, her body trimmed with feminine muscle, sleek and compact—her skin flawless and flushed pink. Vibrant, beautiful.

"No." She'd whispered the word, but only after his gaze had dropped to her lips, catching their slight tremor.

"Why?" he snarled, more to himself because he found no satisfaction in the fear that quivered her chin, brittled the blue of her eyes. "Tell me."

"It wasn't your problem."

The agony of the past years surged into fury and disbelief, heating his temper. Revenge was not only sweet, it was justifiable. One hand snaked out, gripped her hair while the other held her in place. He wasn't gentle, couldn't have been if he wanted. She slammed into him, her gasp of denial hovering just below his mouth.

A bullet splintered the wood pane behind his shoulder, cutting off Cain's retribution with a jerk of his head.

In unison, they dove around the curve, hitting the iron walkway hard. "Go!" Cain shouted in her ear but she was already moving, crawling around the curve.

He grabbed his gun from its holster. Holding it barrel up, he tilted his head and peered over the low wall that surrounded the lamp room. "The shot came from the trees." His words were curt, snapped out over another burst of gunfire.

"This isn't your battle, Cain." Celeste reached down, snagged the small 9mm from her back, ignoring the trembling in her hands. Damn it, she'd left him because of this. She tried not to think of how close his mouth had come to hers—the overwhelming temptation to close the distance herself.

"That's where you're wrong. It became mine the second those bullets hit Mercer's stomach." Another shot ricocheted, this time mere inches from Celeste's ear. Cursing, Cain pressed her farther onto the iron walkway. "Keep your head down!"

In the summer, the windows around the lighthouse were curtained during the day to eliminate the sun. Otherwise, the lens became a giant magnifying glass strong enough to start fires in the surrounding scrub. Unfortunately for her and Cain, the county's historical society removed the curtains for the winter. The open panels of glass would make them easy targets for the sniper.

She nodded in the general direction of the woods. "That second shot came from the top of the trail, about sixty yards. He's got us pinned."

He glanced through the metal railing, judging the

distance. His eyes met hers. Cold-hard slate clashed against azure hued steel. "So we jump."

She assessed the hundred-foot drop, only sparing a brief glimpse at the water pounding the rocks and sand below. "I see you haven't lost your warped sense of humor."

"Now sweetheart, you know I prefer the term *dry,*" Cain answered, the sarcasm deadly.

Simultaneously, they fired off several shots into the closest bank of trees. The glass panel exploded over their heads, Cain grunted. "Nothing humorous about this guy." He released the empty magazine, then shoved it into his coat pocket.

"He's playing with us, Cain."

"And he's alone. Wouldn't be any fun otherwise." Cain shoved a new magazine into his pistol. "How many clips do you have?"

"One more," Celeste admitted. She fired while he reloaded, knowing twelve bullets wouldn't give them much time.

"Even if we had a hundred, our range is much shorter." He snapped the buckle from his belt. "Up for a little rappelling?" Encased in the metal was a long thin wire-like cable and miniature grappling hook.

"Is that safe?"

"Worried?"

Yes. "Curious."

He quirked his eyebrow then, she saw the twitch at his lips. She found herself wanting to see him smile and that annoyed her.

Quickly he uncoiled the cable. "Kate's latest project.

Synthetic spider silk. Stronger than steel cable, flexible like nylon."

Celeste knew who Kate was of course. The female version of Cain, with raven hair and slate-gray eyes. She'd met Doctor Kate MacAlister, now D'Amato, briefly at a dinner party for some Washington senator, long before she'd met Cain actually. Damn smart, she remembered—and that from nothing more than a shake of hands, and a few polite sentences.

A world-renowned scientist, Kate was the youngest of the over-achieving MacAlister siblings, Cain being the eldest with their brother, Ian, filling the middle.

Celeste glanced at the ground before slipping her gun back into its holster. "You have a hundred feet worth of twine in there?"

"Twenty," he corrected before refastening his belt and hooking the end of the rope to the railing. "Enough to get us to the first window below." Within seconds, he'd removed his coat and handed it to her. "The leather will protect you better against flying glass. Use your heels to kick in the window."

"And the stray bullets?" Keeping low, she shrugged into his jacket. She caught the scent of leather, soap and moisture—as if he'd just bathed in the icy waters of Lake Huron. An overwhelming urge to snuggle into the warmth surged through her.

"Won't touch us if we do it right." Quickly, he threaded the wire into a makeshift harness between her legs before clipping it around her waist. "It's weighted to hold me plus another two hundred pounds."

His gaze raked over her. "You've lost weight. Almost too much."

"But you haven't lost that MacAlister charm," she murmured. At five foot three, Celeste never had tipped the scales much over a hundred and fifteen pounds, but secretly, even she admitted it'd been months since she'd come close.

"You'll be okay." He reached into the pocket of his jacket. A second later he handed her a pair of dark leather gloves. "Once you get through the window, undo the cord and I'll pull it up."

"Thanks," she retorted, not bothering to hide her derision. Instead, she studied the width between the iron railings.

"Don't worry. At my count of three, throw yourself over. I'll cover you."

"And who's going to cover you?"

The hitch in her voice caught his attention. His eyes narrowed. "I'll take care of that, too."

Always the hero. And if he got hurt? What then? Annoyed by the fact that she cared, she slipped on the oversize gloves, the inside pelt still warm from his hand. Her skin tingled but not from nerves. Not this time. "I don't—"

He captured her chin, his fingers firm. "Gypsy, do what you're told."

Her heart stumbled. She caught it in a gasp. Gypsy. She hadn't heard the endearment since their weekend together at his cabin in Colorado, when he'd whispered it, hot and moist, against her ear.

The same weekend he'd proposed.

Cain turned her toward the railing, making sure she was balanced in her crouched position. "One…two…three!"

Gunfire exploded around them. Celeste threw herself at the railing. The hard edge of metal hit just under her ribs, causing her to catch her breath. A searing pain stabbed her side, and she cried out. Suddenly, a hand curved the back of her thigh and hoisted her over the railing.

Rapid fire struck the barrier nearby. A bullet hit Cain's pistol, knocking it from his hand into the water below. Cursing, he curled himself around her, and flung them both over.

The cable shuddered and then tossed them into the wall of the lighthouse. Cain grunted as he slammed into the concrete, back first.

"Hold on." His breath tickled the slope of her neck where her shirt had ridden down. Nerves dried her throat, nothing else, she told herself. If they weren't hanging eighty feet from the ground she probably would've found the situation humorous. He gripped her waist, but Celeste wasn't sure how strong a hold he had. She closed her eyes briefly and prayed.

Twisting, Cain flipped them around. With his feet braced against the wall, he used his upper-body strength and tucked her into the curve of his chest.

"Cover your face." Cain grabbed her gun from its holster. The pistol exploded two rounds. Glass shattered.

With one sharp kick, the window frame snapped. Seconds later, they landed inside.

Despite the chill in the air, drops of sweat tickled the damp skin between her shoulder blades. Senses alert, her gaze scoured the inside of the lighthouse.

Framed by the spiraled stairs hung five hundred pounds of iron. The clockwork weight-driven mechanism had been designed like a cuckoo clock with gears, cable and a large spool. Once the keeper rewound the cable onto the spool by crank, the weight lowered inch by inch into the tower, causing the clamshell-like lens to turn.

"This is the guy who killed Mercer." Cain grabbed her hand and pulled her down the stairs behind him. "And who planted the C-4 explosives in your car." When he stopped at the bottom, she nearly collided with him. "Am I right?"

"I think so. And my guess is he's really pissed off now that he's found out I'm still alive."

Another spray of bullets had him checking out the window, her gun still in his hand. "Just for the record, he's not the only one pissed off about that."

Before she could answer, Cain hit the door with his foot. Wood splintered, then slammed against concrete. Bullets strafed the lighthouse, catching them in the doorway. Celeste dove behind a nearby log, then felt the hard impact of Cain's body beside her. Bullets sprayed the sand around them. Cain fired back, targeting the ridge. "He hasn't moved.

"Give me my gun," she demanded, then took off his gloves and shoved them back into his coat pocket.

"I'm the better shot." He nodded toward the keeper's cottage standing halfway between them and the edge of the woods. "Run on three. I'll cover." His fingers hit the air. "One…two…three!"

Celeste flung herself over the log and hit the ground in a roll, coming up only yards from the small brick cottage. Gunfire raged around her, peppering her path. Adrenaline surged as she dug into the sand for traction. It sucked at her feet, weighing them down. *Too slow. You're running too slow.* She dug harder until her calf muscles burned. Suddenly, Cain tackled her from behind, carrying them both several feet through the air. They hit the ground, a yard from the cottage wall.

Bits of frozen sand scratched her eyes. She tried to blink the sting away, spit the grit from her mouth. "I would've made it," she snapped, then tried to wiggle out of his hold. Cain's body tightened, she felt every line, every rigid muscle. Cursing herself when her body softened in response.

Cain hissed. In one fluid motion, he stood and positioned himself flush against the wall. "Only because he was toying with you." Cain's face shifted into tight lines. "Do a better job next time." His gaze caught hers, the message clear, before returning to survey the path. "There's a cluster of rocks ten meters ahead."

She fought the twinge of panic. "Damn it, Cain. If this guy is Jonathon's killer, did it occur to you that he wants me and that maybe, just maybe, you might be in the way?"

"That's the plan." He handed her the gun. "Do you think you can cover me?"

"Try me." Celeste gripped her gun tightly, her sweaty palm slick against the steel. For two cents, she might just shoot him and his condescending attitude. With a shove, she reloaded her weapon, satisfied when the clip snapped into place. "I'd take the bike path to your left, it comes out behind the ridge. Might give you an advantage." She nodded toward the path, nestled in the trees across about twenty feet of sand to their left. "But you'd better run fast. I've only got a few rounds left," she snapped and scanned the beach, not totally convinced this sniper was alone. "And I might shoot you by accident."

"Then aim at the sky," Cain ordered before he hit the ground running toward the woods. "And stay put."

With a precision that belied the tremble in her fingers, Celeste emptied the clip into the ridge as the dense pines swallowed him whole. In the distance, rifle fire strafed the woods in response.

She scoured the terrain until her eyes ached. But the shadows grew longer, their depths murky.

Nothing.

Adrenaline fed her. That and fear. After all this, she couldn't lose him now. Wouldn't. With grim determination, Celeste darted after Cain, empty gun in hand.

Understanding one way or another, she'd pay.

Chapter Three

"What the hell were you thinking?" Cain met her at the top of the trail, his rage palpable.

"I don't know," she snapped, her tone sarcastic, her nerves crackling from the adrenaline that came from picturing Cain dead. "Maybe that you'd get your ass shot off if I didn't back you up."

His eyes narrowed at the cussing. In the past, Diana had never cussed. Well, that was just too damned bad, she wasn't Diana anymore. The sooner he realized that the better.

"And how would you manage to save my *ass?* By pitching your pistol at a rifle and taking it out?" He grabbed her hand and dropped some cartridges into her palm. "Fifty-caliber. Think you could've stopped one of those?"

"At least I had something." Her chin tilted in defiance, her fist closed around the metal, hoping to gain some control. Now wasn't the time to tell him she'd never been on the wrong end of the gun.

"I had something too." Within a blink, a knife appeared in Cain's hand and in the next breath it was sheathed once more inside his sleeve. So he still carried it. A present from her; in its high-carbon steel she'd had engraved the word *Prometheus*.

An engine gunned in the distance. Cain bit out a curse. In unison, they bolted toward Cain's Jag, parked a few yards away, as Cain punched the car remote, unlocking its doors. "He's headed north toward town," Cain yelled.

"Don't tell me—your little voice?" She reached the door, then jerked it open and was caught off guard when the scent of leather hit her. She hesitated, but only for the second she needed to forestall the nausea. A reaction she'd dealt with ever since Gram's death. Ignoring his lifted eyebrow, she asked, "Is that voice of yours still foolproof?"

"It didn't tell me you were alive." Celeste scrambled in, just as Cain slammed his door and turned the ignition. Tires squealed as he stomped on the accelerator. "Press the white button under your seat."

When she did, a slim drawer slid out, its contents two 9mm Glocks and a dozen clips.

When she quirked her brow, he answered. "The car is a prototype."

"Your sister keeps busy, doesn't she?" Celeste grabbed both pistols, checked them and handed him one.

"She's pregnant. As a scientist, developing safeguards channels her mothering instinct into something productive." He placed the Glock on his lap.

Celeste caught the thread of pride that ran through his statement. The sibling bond. A pang of envy tightened her stomach. Being an only child, she'd never experienced that kind of closeness. "You mean, now that she's pregnant, her maternal instinct is to find ways to protect her brother from harm."

"Exactly."

"And Roman? Is he still in the business now that's he's going to be a father?" The importance of the question resonated through Celeste.

He shot her a look. "For a dead woman, you're pretty well informed."

When Celeste didn't answer, he said. "Roman retired from the agency once he married Kate and now he runs my company." For years, Cain's company, MacAlister Securities, had served as a cover for both Cain and Roman. Now it seems the job had become a legitimate one for Roman. Kate wouldn't have to worry about being a widow.

"And the car?"

"It's loaded with the latest detection and satellite systems. All reinforced with special plating." He downshifted to take a particularly nasty hairpin turn in the road.

Bombproof. He didn't say it, but she understood. The upgrades had been a direct result of her death. "It wasn't you he'd wanted, Cain. Remember, I'd been driving your car for a month."

"Trying to analyze me?"

Celeste's eyes skimmed the wedge of trees on both sides of the road, spotting nothing except the flash of roadside mailboxes passing by. "It's my job." She propped her elbow on the door rest, and tugged at her hair, not caring if she left the strands in disarray. "We almost had him."

"We might not be out of luck yet." He nodded toward his mirror. She caught a dark green sedan maneuvering behind them. When it signaled to pass, Cain automatically slowed a bit.

"You think he waited off the road somewhere for us to pass?" Celeste noted the tinted windows just before it came abreast of theirs.

Cain tightened his grip on the steering wheel and shifted the Jag into high gear. "Hold on!"

The sedan slammed into Cain's side, catching the Jag's back panel. The impact threw Celeste sideways.

The sedan hit again, this time holding tight against them and forcing Cain onto the right shoulder of the road. Bullets pinged their car. Cain hit the gas and jerked the wheel, sending them into the oncoming lane but keeping them in front of the sedan. "Close your eyes, Gypsy."

"Don't tell me—" Celeste caught sight of a semi truck, two tons of chrome and steel, bearing down on them with its horn blaring and called herself an idiot for not taking Cain's advice. "Watch out!"

Chapter Four

"Trust me." Cain downshifted and hit the road's left shoulder. "I've got it under control."

Shots hit the back windshield leaving several webbed cracks in the glass. Celeste ducked, a major feat while her eyes remained glued to the sedan closing the distance. "I hope so, because he's coming again."

"Grab something!" Cain roared.

He didn't need to tell her twice. Alarm shot down her spine, pooling at its base. Celeste grabbed the dashboard seconds before Cain plowed through some roadside mailboxes.

When the Jag hit the pavement, he wrenched the steering wheel and hit the brake, sending the car into a nasty spin. Celeste's cry drowned under the screech of tires.

Cain jumped from the car, his gun appearing in his hand. He slammed the door shut. "Stay down!"

It wasn't until later she realized she'd ignored his order again. Cain crouched, his gun low, deliberately waiting. Her heart threatened to explode. She hit her seat belt release, grabbed her gun then scrambled out her side, using the car as a barrier.

Her breath came in shallow, quick gasps as the sedan bore down on them. Systematically she and Cain fired, emptying their guns into the car as it sped by.

"Get in!" Cain leaped back into the Jag, his expression dark with an unreadable emotion as she followed. He hit the accelerator and gravel flew, pelting the car.

But when they rounded the next curve, the sedan had disappeared. Too many side roads and winding driveways all covered with snow that effectively blocked any dirt from kicking up made it impossible to determine his escape route. Cain skidded to a stop, his eyes searching, knowing that in the darkness, the chase was useless. He jammed the car into Park.

"Next time." Cain's expression hardened. Only the systematic flexing of his fingers on the steering wheel told Celeste how angry he was.

"Are you crazy?" Fury drove her. That and terror. He'd done it, she thought. His indifference to danger had taken her beyond control. Later she'd figure what do about it, but for right now she'd use what wits she had left to yell. "Do you think those bullets were made out of marshmallows? One of them could've hit you and you'd be dead. Even I know you don't stand out in the middle of a road and let some idiot use you for target practice."

"Bullet-proof." Briefly, Cain tugged at his shirt before dismissing her without a second glance. "I know what I'm doing."

"You've got to be kidding!" Celeste squeezed his arm, maybe a little harder than necessary, but she didn't care. It annoyed her he'd said the words so casually. The lean muscle beneath her fingers flexed, showing its strength, forcing her to concentrate on the material. She wouldn't give him the satisfaction of flinging herself into his arms, holding him tight.

Not while she was bawling him out.

"He could've been firing armor-piercing bullets," she admonished, using the shirt as a pretext to assure herself that he was all right. The cotton material appeared no different from any other.

She glanced down. "The jacket, too?"

"Yes." She should've known when he'd insisted she wear it at the lighthouse earlier.

"The lining is specifically woven with a newly developed bullet-proof material. Kate has been working on a process for some time." He flipped the jacket's collar back and forth. "The weight difference in the cloth is minimal." His knuckles brushed her cheek, sending a cascade of goose bumps over her skin. Her reaction just fed her anger.

"Another MacAlister gadget?" Intuitively, Celeste knew Kate wouldn't be happy about Cain's recent stunt either. "It's probably the only way she can counter your heroics."

"It holds a ninety-percent effectiveness rating," Cain commented, unaware of Celeste's thoughts. "Enough to put the odds in my favor."

She let the ten-percent difference slide because she had bigger fish to fry. "What about your head? Last I heard *stupidity* was many things, but it wasn't bullet-proof."

"A calculated risk. If he wanted us dead now, he wouldn't have given up so easily at the lighthouse."

Cain grabbed his cell phone, pressed the key pad and put the receiver to his ear. "And he would've hit me with at least one bullet just now. He took Jon Mercer out from eight hundred yards with a double tap to his stomach."

"That's a big if." His indifference pushed her into rage. "And here's another. If a ricochet had hit you by mistake, you'd have been just as dead."

Cain held up his hand to stop her tirade. "Ian, I need a make. Dark gray. Taurus. License plate Charlie, Tango, Alpha—that's all I got."

Cain's younger brother, Ian, was an ex-navy SEAL. Jon had mentioned to Celeste that he'd resigned his commission. Obviously, he was working for Cain. "I don't believe this. The next time you stand up in the open against an armed assassin, I'll help Kate make you an armored straitjacket."

She'd muttered the words, but he heard.

"Hold on, Ian." He reached over and caught her chin. "The next time you don't stay when I tell you to, Gypsy, you'll have the opportunity. Because I'll lock you up tight in a little room right next to her lab."

Celeste slapped his hand down, telling herself she'd do the same to Cain when this was finished.

"Ian, the car's probably stolen, but let me know. I want this guy." Cain's eyes narrowed into twin blades of tempered steel so sharp they left Celeste no escape as they sliced through the car. "Let's just say, we played a little chicken today."

With those words, she hugged herself, finally understanding what he hadn't told her. This went beyond finding Mercer's killer, beyond duty.

This was personal.

"It was a draw."

She heard the promise in his answer.

"This time."

ON THE RIDE back to town, Celeste managed to temper the swell of anxiety that rose through her. It wasn't the killer who scared her, not overtly anyway. She wasn't stupid— she knew the man was dangerous—but she'd waited too long to let a simple warning from him make her bolt.

No, the killer didn't frighten her half as much as Cain did.

Logic dictated they join forces to find Mercer's killer, but she'd discovered the hard way that logic sometimes didn't matter.

"What the hell was Jon thinking?"

Irritated, she didn't pretend not to understand the question. "Maybe that I could take care of myself."

"You're a profiler, not a trained undercover operative."

"You make it sound like it was an assignment. Or worse, one that I had asked for."

"Look, Jon saw something in you. Something no one else did. I won't deny that." The both knew that during her mid twenties, she had shown a natural talent for profiling. Enough that one of her professors recruited her into the FBI's program in Quantico, Virginia. Within a few years, at the urge of President Cambridge, Jonathon had approached her to join Labyrinth.

"I quit Labyrinth right before the car bomb. Jonathon didn't have much say in my decision."

"He told me at your gravesite. Look…" Cain sighed.

"I can't change the past. Or my decision to stay in Colombia while you were under investigation for the Bobby Cambridge murder. But I'm here now." He cocked his head, arched an eyebrow. "Want to talk about it?"

Celeste would've gone with the quick, decisive no response. The one she'd repeated a thousand times. Mostly to a set of government psychologists whose job it had been to determine her sanity.

Except that she'd caught the quiet understanding that shadowed his features.

How many times during her ordeal, had she wished for this moment? How many times, with her spirit nearly shredded by lies, had she begged God to bring Cain to her rescue?

But he'd chosen to stay on assignment, even when Mercer had sent for him. Knowing Cain, she hadn't expected anything else. Loving Cain, she'd hoped for more.

Shame snapped her spine to attention. Pride kept it straight. He hadn't come then, couldn't, but still she had hoped. "They prepare you in training, condition you for possible capture and enemy interrogations." She gripped her hands, concentrating on the tinge of pain rather than the echoes of humiliation. "They just never tell you that sometimes, they turn out to be the enemy themselves."

"I wasn't your enemy, Celeste." His grim tone only deepened the sadness of the memory. "I was on the verge of a major arms bust, people were going to die, if it hadn't been vital—"

"You'd have been with me." Her voice sounded strained even to her ears. "I understood that."

"Did you? Mercer told me you wouldn't let him explain why I'd decided to stay." She studied the stone-hewed features beside her. When his mouth tightened, she caught the slight gesture only because she was looking so hard. She suspected he didn't care whether she observed him or not and that the grim line was more for her benefit than because of his thoughts.

It was amazing, she thought. Indifferent, even stoic—the man still dripped sex. But it had always been that way, ever since the moment she'd first met him years before.

"You were on assignment, Cain. The details of that mission wouldn't have changed the outcome of my situation. Or my career with the agency."

Ironically, the same career that had brought them together, she mused. Roman had set up their first meeting at MacAlister Securities, on a case Celeste could no longer recall clearly. Cain had arrived in a tuxedo. He'd been on his way to some kind of reception, she remembered, but she'd caught the sudden shift from indifference to curiosity when Roman introduced them. It wasn't until his hand brushed hers in a handshake, that time had slowed. Ever so slightly, he'd caressed her wrist, catching the flutter beneath his thumb. When his eyes had caught hers, their smoky depths swirled with hidden promises—promises that had sparked a fire deep within her belly. And others, she found in the deeper, calmer layers of gray that warmed her heart.

With a single phone call, his schedule had been rearranged, his dinner engagement forgotten. Suddenly their brief encounter turned into an intimate supper, the wine to an expensive bottle of champagne. The hand-shake to feather-light touches and responding sighs...

"Labyrinth or not, Jon should've placed you under protection—"

"Someone high in the ranks contracted this killer. No one can be trusted."

"I could've damn well protected you."

"Your choice," she snapped, then immediately regretted it. "Look, it was better that you didn't. You would've hidden me away, then gone after him yourself."

"Damn right."

"And you would've died. No one was safe with me, Gram's death proved that. I insisted on disappearing alone." Celeste felt her anger rise and tried to beat it down. "I didn't give Jonathon a choice."

"And he's dead."

"That's it, isn't it?" It wasn't the words that caught her attention, but the animosity underneath. "You're angry. But what are you angry about, Cain? That you decided to bring down an arms dealer rather than hold my hand through an investigation?"

"The investigation was standard procedure. The car bomb wasn't."

"So it's because Jonathon didn't tell you I'd survived."

"Not Jon. You."

"I'd already decided I wasn't going to marry you. Telling you I was alive made no sense."

When he didn't deny it, she said, "You think it was an easy decision?"

"Which? Breaking the engagement or not letting me know you were alive?"

"Both." Celeste answered, allowing the bitterness to filter through. "You didn't love me. The engagement was a mistake that I had no intention of compounding by involving you in this mess."

"Engagement or not, you shouldn't have run from me." This time the rage was there, simmering under every syllable, thickening the air between them. "You should've damn well run *to me* for help."

"And what could you have done that Jonathon hadn't?" she asked with disdain, not waiting for an answer. Cain hadn't denied her accusation that he'd never loved her. The realization made her throat ache. "One of these days you're going to trip over your arrogance, Cain."

"Tread carefully, Gypsy. Because my arrogance isn't what you should be worried about right now."

But it was too late for that. The fear, the injustice, the years of guilt converged on her in one fell swoop, overpowering any thought of prudence. She leaned in, wanting him to see what he'd stirred in her—how much she resented it. "You know why, you weren't told? Why you weren't brought in to protect me after Grams died?" Her finger hit his bicep with each question, not caring when she found steel beneath, her emotions no more under control than a runaway train.

"No. Why don't you tell me."

Determined to, she missed the flash of heat behind his eyes, the threat in his tone. "It's because the mission was on a need-to-know basis. And for once, MacAlister, you weren't on the list."

He jammed the brake, bringing the car to a dead stop

on the roadside. The force threw her forward, then snapped her back like a rubber band. Before she could react, he'd hit the clip of her seatbelt, caught her shoulders in a vice grip and jerked her to him. Her heart slammed into her ribs, her teeth knocked together.

"Damn you!" Then his lips hit hers, punishing. No love, no desire.

A reckoning—to her, for the agony of what she'd put him through, and to him, for allowing himself to suffer.

Not what she'd remembered, not what she'd realized she wanted. Desire bubbled, touched off by the heat of temper, like molten lava that had been waiting a century to awaken. With it, came the quakes of uncertainty, the tremors of fear.

Don't make it worse, she told herself. Don't make it genuine.

His mouth shifted, as if sensing the surge of emotion. The tempest settled into something deeper, but no less dangerous. Just more confusing.

She wouldn't struggle.

As it turned out, she couldn't.

With a few strokes of his tongue against her lips, the confusion became curiosity, the curiosity, yearning. All within a heartbeat. Her mouth opened on a gasp as the hunger slammed into her emotions, hurling her off balance.

Then he pushed her away. But not far enough for her to feel safe. She jerked back, crying out when her head smacked the window. She blinked, angry enough to say something, cautious enough to hold her tongue.

He gunned the engine, taking out his rage on the machine. Without a word, she settled into her seat, aware of the nearness of his body, the deafening silence.

The persistent sting in her scalp didn't register until he turned onto the road. But she didn't rub away the pain. Instead, she hugged her chest, tight—the ache in her heart hurting far worse.

"Here." Cain reached into his jeans pocket and withdrew five quarters. "We were at Kate's wedding reception. Jon had joined me on the hotel balcony to smoke a cigar just before he was shot."

"Brand new." Celeste moved closer, hating the nervousness that crept in, and glanced at the backs of the coins. The State of Michigan. "All identical."

"All in an envelope inside Jon's pocket. No prints, of course. Nothing but Mercer's name. Laser printed." Cain paused long enough to slide a glance her way. "These were a present from Jon's killer."

Celeste nodded. "It's his trademark. Which means Jon's killer would've been at the reception disguised as a waiter, a guest. Anyone," she reasoned aloud. "If the coins had been slipped into his pocket any earlier, Jonathon would have discovered them and would've notified me or taken better precautions."

"Possibly." For a moment, Cain's gaze didn't leave Celeste's face, unnerving her. What did he think he'd see? Carefully, she schooled her expression.

"Either way, the hit man was making a statement."

"No, not a statement," she corrected, then took the quarters and examined them one by one in the light of the window. "The coins tell us that the killer knew I was in Michigan before he shot Jonathon. He was issuing a challenge."

"Lucky for him I'm listening then."

"It wasn't luck, Cain. If I'm right, this guy knew exactly which buttons to push to bring you here."

"Then we'll just have to start pushing back."

"Define *we*," she countered.

"*We* don't need to be lovers, Gypsy. Or friends." It was a statement of fact. Spoken bluntly. "We just have to be in agreement. Either I'm in or you're out."

"Meaning?" She shifted, instantly alert, unwilling to be caught off guard again.

"It would only take one phone call for me to arrange for your protection," he challenged.

"Which, defined by your terms, isn't really protection, but more like…imprisonment," she replied, her jaw clenched. Cain never threw out idle threats—the fact his taste still lingered on her lips was proof.

"Can't fool you. But then I've always said you were good at your job." Cain downshifted to avoid a squirrel in the road, not surprising Celeste. "If I think it's for your own good, I'll have men here in less than an hour with an arrest warrant."

"I'm sure there's a compliment somewhere in there," she answered derisively, not willing to give him the satisfaction of knowing she caught the grin that played over his lips.

Jerk.

"Even if you could trust them, Cain, it would be impossible." Having her arrested that quickly would take resources that Cain didn't have access to—

She jolted with the realization. Jon had only been dead a day, but it was still feasible. She'd heard the rumors, even before she'd left. Nothing overt, just the whispers. The great Prometheus. The only man who could take over the reins of Labyrinth when Mercer retired. "You're the temporary director, aren't you?"

"The jury's still out," he answered, seemingly unsurprised by her comment. "Mine and theirs."

"You'll take the job." She moved away, suddenly needing the distance a few inches put between them. "And the truth is, you *should* become the new director. And Jon realized it."

"My coming here had nothing to do with being director and everything to do with Jon's murder and you."

Cain maneuvered the Jag onto Shadow Point's main street. The wind kicked up, rattling the wooden signs of the storefronts. Celeste caught sight of the white clapboard buildings, most painted the previous summer, some showing signs of movement inside.

Not a surprise, even for Saturday night. For the last week or so, most owners spent hours after closing preparing for the Cambridge Charity auction, knowing the town would receive an early influx of tourists.

"Do we have a deal?" His access to information made it impossible for her to object and they both knew it.

"On one condition." She pointed out the car window to the few people on the sidewalk. The residents' easy acceptance, their unabashed friendliness, had soothed her shattered soul, then eventually, had won her heart and her loyalty. "See them?" Her index finger tapped the window, not caring that she left smudges on the glass.

"There's a good chance they're in danger and don't even know it. I refuse to let that happen."

"It wouldn't happen if we put you somewhere safe." He parked in front of her store and shut off the engine.

"No. He'd find me, Cain. Then other people would get hurt in the process." *You.* Celeste deliberately faced Cain, her back straight, her jaw tight. "I want Mercer's killer found. I want the guy who thinks he can take pot shots at me and get away with it caught. Then I want you far away from me as soon as possible. Agreed?"

After a long, torturous moment, Cain punched a button and unlocked the door. "Agreed."

"Partners," she muttered, not bothering to hide her annoyance as she followed him onto the pavement.

"Not quite." He slipped the keys into his pocket before giving them a careless jingle. "You're not experienced enough."

"What?"

His comment rankled. Or maybe it was stubborn line of his lips.

"This isn't up for debate." He took in the damage to the Jag, then he pointed to the barely dented metal. "You're still in trouble. If he knows where you run, he knows where you live."

Trouble she could handle. Cain, she wasn't so sure about. Celeste eyed the minor dents and scratches. Obviously, he'd told her the truth about the car having reinforced plating. Just like its owner. Celeste watched him for a moment. "How did you know to find me at the lighthouse?"

"I followed you." The negligent lift of his shoulder

seemed almost too casual. "Which is why we're going to relocate you."

"I'm not leaving my home. I have responsibilities."

Cain froze, his eyes murderous, startling her. With a long glance at her stomach, he asked, "What responsibilities?"

Chapter Five

"What? You think I have a baby?" The quiver in her belly stayed out of her voice, just barely. Celeste couldn't deny that in those first weeks, she'd hoped, even prayed for what might be.

Then later she'd dreamed, knowing it would never be.

"Relax, Cain. My responsibilities include the feline kind. My cat, Pan."

"A cat is portable."

"My antique business isn't." He raised an eyebrow. She quirked hers right back.

Diana Taylor had taken pride in not being tied down to anyone or anything until she'd met Cain. She'd lived from hotel to hotel, never forming roots. A gypsy, he'd called her until it had become an endearment.

"I see."

"No, you don't, but that's okay." She jabbed her thumb at the Jag's back window. "Shouldn't we move the car to the alley?"

"No," he said, not bothering to follow her gaze. "If anyone asks, tell them a flock of irate seagulls attacked us."

"Oh, for heaven's sake." She folded her arms to keep from shaking him in frustration. The man was turning her into a loon. "No one's going to believe that."

"It doesn't matter whether they believe it or not." He tugged on her coat sleeve, pulling her along the sidewalk. "It's time to eat and talk."

"Fine." She clutched her collar together, giving in to a sudden need to protect herself. "You eat. I'll talk."

"I believe, Gypsy, we're finally communicating."

"If you think this is communicating," she copied his dry tone, pleased with herself when she succeeded. "We're in for a rough time."

DIANA *had* changed. And the evidence proved to be her business, Cain decided.

The sun had lost its intensity, sliding farther toward the horizon. Within an hour it would be dark. Already heavy with the promise of snow, the evening breeze tugged at their coats and nipped at their ears.

Diana's store stood alone in a two-story building at the end of town. Only the whitewash and green trim showed any similarity to the other stores which stood in a long curvy tail bordering Main Street.

Cain noticed the sign first, only because of the squawk of the hinges as it swung in the wind. "A Touch of Serenity. Is that just your store's name or a goal?"

"It's my home."

A home, he knew, she struggled to keep. It had taken very little effort to pull her financial records. Within hours, Roman had given him a detailed report of her bank accounts—which held barely enough for her to live on.

A line of benches marched along the boardwalk, all black wrought iron with green slats of wood, all flanked by sandstone flowerpots and all strategically separated by matching garbage containers.

Except in front of Diana's place. Her porch was subtly different. *Cozy* came to mind, startling Cain. With a bay window for its backdrop, a swing bench hung to the right of the door while two rockers sat on the left flanked by wooden barrels, big enough to hold a morning coffee or a set of feet for a lunchtime nap.

"A little cold to be sitting outside, don't you think?"

"I like to rock." She glanced at the bench before putting her key into the lock. "On a good night when the stars shine, I like the cold, too."

Cain almost grinned at that, remembering a time when the slightest breeze would send Diana into a fit of shivers. A woman couldn't change that much.

It only took one glance at the inside of her store to prove him wrong.

If *cozy* described the porch, the warm, Victorian charm of the store put *cozy* to shame.

He'd known it was an antique store, and he'd been in many, shopping with his mother, dragged along by his sister. Both were antique fanatics. But Cain had never seen one like Diana's.

Couches and chairs—some in pastel florals, others in jewel-colored velvets in blue, green and gold—crowded the floor, setting off the dark grain of the hardwood. Groomed and overstuffed, each piece set to draw the eye to the softer tones of vintage oak, mahogany and cherrywood furniture nestled nearby. Fragile lace throws and hand-crocheted doilies covered every piece.

"Nice place, Gypsy." An oversize stone fireplace stood to the right, waiting patiently with fresh logs to light.

Celeste threw the dead bolt, punched in her ten-digit code, and waited impatiently for the red light to beep. "You sound surprised."

"Considering that only a few years ago, the idea of staying more than a month at one particular hotel got on your nerves, yes, I am surprised," he admitted.

"I told you before, that was Diana, Cain. Not me. I enjoy collecting pieces of the past for my customers."

Simple solution, for someone who has to live without one, Cain thought. "You got the full security package, didn't you? Motion, heat, the debugging sensor. Not top of the line—not even close—but workable."

"Jonathon insisted on the security." Her voice remained even. "I insisted that it wouldn't be one of your systems." She flipped on the overhead track lights. They cast a soft, easy glow across crystal decanters and stained-glass lamps, leaving one's mind with a nostalgic sense of the past. "If our killer shows up, we'll know it."

Cain caught the light scent of rose and talcum that was Diana's grandmother.

Another deliberate reminder?

She yanked off his coat and tossed it onto a hundred-odd-year-old oak chest. Her mouth thinned. "I've brought home a guest, Pan." Eyes a few shades lighter than Diana's own blue ones studied Cain from the top of an eight-foot-tall antique library shelf.

The sleek black cat yawned in response, a full, wide yawn that allowed his pink tongue to unroll leisurely from his mouth.

Celeste smiled wickedly at Cain. "He doesn't seem impressed."

"That makes two of you," he mused. "Had him long?"

"Since I moved in. He came with the place. I found him in the storage room while I was unpacking." She held out her arms and Pan jumped into them. "I realized soon after that I enjoyed his company." Cain watched intrigued as Celeste rubbed her cheek against the cat's head, then whispered something soothing in his ear.

Pan jumped from her arms and she laughed. "My company he takes in small doses." For a moment, she watched Pan relocate on the bay window's overstuffed cushion and stretch out. "He has his own entrance through the stock room for his midnight prowls. An old dryer vent near the floor. It's no bigger than his head, so I don't worry too much about someone else squeezing through." With a shake of her head, she said, "Sometimes I really envy his independence."

For a response, Cain sauntered over and scratched Pan between the ears. "Hello, cat."

With a long, lazy purr, Pan flipped over on his back and started batting his paws at Cain's hand.

Celeste frowned over the male bonding.

"Any other…friends I should know about?"

"You never used to play games, Cain. I'm sure within seconds after locating me, you had Roman do a background check."

Cain straightened, ending his game with Pan. "Only

what we could find out through data bases." Cain's tone was tolerant as he eyed a small musical figurine on a nearby lace-covered table. The statuette was of a young woman rocking a small, sleeping boy, his head snuggled against her shoulder. He picked up the figurine and wound the key. The low tinkling of a lullaby filled the air. "I like this."

Handcrafted in Italy, the figurine was a favorite of hers too. Actually, she loved it. So much, she'd been tempted to keep it herself. But why did the fact he liked it too suddenly anger her?

"There's no special person in your life right now?"

"No one." Her chin tilted enough to show off the stubbornness. "Loving someone would only risk their life."

A yowl mocked her from across the room. "Shut up, Pan."

Cain cleared what might have been the beginning of a laugh from his throat. "I take it he doesn't want to be excluded."

"Most likely," she lied, conscious of the flush that invaded her cheeks.

Cain studied her for a moment but Celeste didn't back down. She had nothing to hide when it came to relationships. The fact that she'd wanted to ask him the same thing, but couldn't without being obvious, only added another layer to her frustration. "Do you want to hear about this killer or not?" she asked, becoming downright angry when the bite in her question only raised an amused eyebrow.

"Isn't that why we're here?"

"I thought so until a moment ago." Now that she was

committed, she wanted to get the job done and get Cain out of her hair. "It started with Bobby Cambridge's murder. More accurately, it started on the day of the kidnapping. Bobby was on his way to a private summer day camp with the usual security detail of Secret Service agents."

Celeste replayed the scene in her mind as her hands kept busy rearranging white roses in a fluted vase. Long-stem roses were the one extravagance she indulged in. "Except one had turned greedy."

"Frank Bremer," Cain responded. "Weapons specialist turned agent after a stint in the military and FBI. A loner. No close friendships, no letters from home. A man who decided to take care of his own retirement."

Celeste's eyes narrowed with suspicion before she continued. "After pulling over for feigned car trouble on a deserted part of the highway, Bremer killed several agents in cold blood, then took off with Bobby."

"Risky," Cain acknowledged. "But Bremer had the element of surprise on his side."

"Exactly. And who else would know Secret Service procedures better?" she asked rhetorically, her hands stopping as she got lost in relating the facts. "He ditched the car for another hidden nearby. By the time back up arrived a few minutes later, he was long gone."

The warmth of the store did nothing to diffuse the cold pit in her stomach. She'd gone over this a hundred times. Still, it never got easier. "It was simple at that point," she said. "Bremer had cut out the tracking chip implanted behind Bobby's ear and left it crushed on the pavement. A few hours later, he made his demands, short and to the point. Then ditched his phone.

"Our guys weren't so smart." Celeste frowned. "After agreeing to the drop-off, the FBI, Secret Service and everyone else involved tried to pull a fast one."

Cain nodded. "Bremer found out—presumably through a phone call from you—went back and killed the kid, then himself. Unusual, but understandable considering we would've hunted him down."

The memory of her grabbing Jonathon, trying to convince him Bremer hadn't worked alone, flashed through her. It was her persistence that had turned their suspicions to her. That and the record of Bremer's number on her cell phone. "It was the official version, yes." Annoyance chewed at her throat, forcing her to clear it. "But not the correct one."

"Okay," Cain said, and then leaned a hip against a nearby sideboard. "Why don't you tell me your version."

"The correct version, you mean."

He folded his arms. "Your version."

The attitude angered her more than the words. "Frank Bremer was smart. He wanted untraceable cash, old bills in small denominations. If they'd even thought about using the standard tricks like dye explosives or tracking devices in the payoff bag, he would've killed Bobby. A helicopter was to drop the money into the Potomac at his specified location with no surveillance. Most figured he would show up in underwater gear and snag the money. But the Feds screwed up. Broke their deal."

Cain's mouth flat-lined. "We don't negotiate with terrorists, even when the president's kid is involved."

"I know, I took National Security 101," Celeste responded derisively. "The FBI kept a twenty-four-hour watch on the drop point. Bremer supposedly found out about it and never showed."

"He'd been updated on all the latest surveillance equipment." Cain crossed his ankles, seemingly relaxed. Celeste knew better. The lines of his body might have eased, but underneath, the muscles remained tense, alert. "Other than the record of his cell number on your phone, there was no evidence of a breach from the inside."

"But it's there. Somewhere." It wasn't easy under Cain's penetrating gaze, but she held her ground. "The point is, by the time the good guys realized Bremer had outmaneuvered them, Bobby was already dead and someone had left Bremer's phone number on my cell. And that someone contracted the hit on Bobby."

"Okay, so Bremer never showed at the drop," Cain continued, obviously aware of the details. "Instead, he went back to the cabin where he'd stashed Bobby and killed the boy with an injection of sodium pentobarbital, then shot himself in the head. End of story, tragic but not unusual in kidnapping cases. Most victims die within the first forty-eight hours—Bobby lived twice that long. And from all accounts, Bremer had treated him well. Some say the boy never saw the end coming."

"My argument exactly and one that ended up biting me in the butt later." Celeste struggled to keep any emotion from underlining her words. "I was on the case from the moment Bobby was kidnapped. I'd insisted on it." If she'd just been less confident, and quicker at putting the pieces together…

"I'm surprised Jon approved the assignment, considering the fact that Grace and Olivia Cambridge were friends."

"He had no choice once President Cambridge requested my help," she said, waving the comment off with her hand.

"So how did Bobby's treatment help your theory?"

"Frank Bremer would never have treated Bobby kindly." She ran her fingers impatiently through her hair. "During his assignment to Bobby, he wasn't friendly or unfriendly, just indifferent. He never complained about the detail, but his associates said that a few weeks before the kidnapping there was always a thinly veiled undertone when he talked about the kid—which wasn't often. Deep down, I'm sure, Bremer considered anything other than protecting the president a step back in his career." Celeste paused, knowing the next portion would burn like salt in wounds yet to heal.

"Don't stop now, Gypsy," he prompted softly. "You're on a roll. After Bremer was assigned to Bobby…"

She nodded, using the few seconds to gather her nerve. "From here it gets a little complicated. Bobby was a sensitive kid. Shy. Introverted. A problem when you happen to be the president's youngest child and your family is continually under the microscope. It only got worse when his sister, Anna, went off to college that first year they were in the White House. The fourteen-year age difference between them made her more of a caregiver than a sister. The same year Anna started college, he started kindergarten. Losing her only added to the stress of facing the attention alone. On his first day of school, Bobby freaked out. To calm him, Olivia gave him an angel coin."

"What kind of coin?"

"A good-luck coin. A Frenchman by the name of Dupré designed the coin in the late 1700s and carried it in his pocket—always," she explained, suddenly aware of the floorboards squeaking. She stopped pacing. "One day, having fallen out of favor with the king, Dupré was arrested. Legend has it that he prayed to his guardian angel—which he'd imprinted on one side of the coin—to save him. Or he could have used it to bribe the guard. Either way, the next day he was set free and the coin became a symbol of good luck."

"A talisman of sorts."

Celeste nodded. "For years, Bobby never went anywhere without that coin in his pocket. It became his security blanket. He'd almost rubbed the image off by using it as a worry stone."

Celeste jammed her fists into her stomach. She'd seen Bobby when they'd found him—had insisted on it. He been sleeping, his body—gangly, with pointed shoulders—tucked endearingly under a NASCAR comforter, similar to those that a thousand boys his age owned. His blond hair was mussed, like that of most ten-year-olds when they are sleeping. The soft spikes of hair were damp against the flushed cheeks—still warm even in death, from dreams of racing, flying jets and space ships.

"Cain, they found the coin in his hand. When Bobby died, I'm positive he wasn't holding the coin. Someone placed it in his right hand later. Deliberately. Bobby was left-handed."

"It only supports the theory that you had profiled Bremer and instructed him exactly how to leave the boy."

"An assassin, not a kidnapper, targeted Bobby. No one could have saved Bobby. By the time I realized it, I'd been set up and Bobby was already dead."

"Only you believed that."

"Cain, Bobby wasn't abused during his captivity. He wasn't restrained, he was well-fed and clean."

Even gripping her fingers together couldn't hide the fact that her hands shook. Cain shifted, fighting the urge to hold her, knowing if he did, she'd fall apart before she could purge the memory. So he did what was necessary, what he seemed to be good at lately. He pushed her temper.

"The FBI experts said only a woman would be that sensitive to the kid…which was one of the things that indicated your involvement."

Chapter Six

"Circumstantial."

He shrugged, satisfied when her eyes fired with anger. "If you say so."

"I do." She started pacing again, but this time the tempo had picked up with determination, her eyes shooting cobalt sparks. Having been raised in a family with Scottish tempers himself, he couldn't miss the flash of fury or the reluctant admiration he felt because of it.

"You're right, Cain. There was no evidence of struggle during those last four days of his life. That showed Bobby trusted his caretaker. At least enough not to fight him. Bobby was the kind of kid who'd have needed constant reassurance from someone he believed in. And since I was with Mercer and a half dozen other guys pretty much during the whole episode, it couldn't have been me."

"Another possibility is that Bremer could've fed Bobby some story—that they were in hiding from some danger, maybe." Cain reasoned. "Gained the kid's trust."

"That scenario doesn't work. Remember Bobby was

an introvert and Bremer had been with him for several months prior to the kidnapping. During that time, there was no friendship, no closeness—only mutual toleration. Top that with the fact Bremer cut up Bobby's ear to get the chip, he wouldn't have trusted Bremer, even if he'd tried to become friends."

"So you're saying it had to be someone new. A Ted Bundy type who was able to gain Bobby's trust almost immediately?"

"Exactly. Almost like a good cop–bad cop ploy."

"With Bremer playing the bad cop," Cain responded grimly.

"Unknowingly, of course. The autopsy showed no outward injuries aside from his ear, not even marks on Bobby's wrists to suggest he was bound. It also indicated that his last meal was a fast-food hamburger and fries. Bremer wouldn't have jeopardized his plans by buying Bobby his favorite meal."

"He could've changed his appearance. Shaved his head, worn a fake goatee."

"All the possible variations of disguises had been sent out over the media and Bobby's disappearance launched the biggest manhunt in two centuries, twentieth and twenty-first. Yet, no one recognized him when he bought the meal? Not likely." Celeste snorted, raising another eyebrow from Cain. God forbid if Diana had done that, she thought.

And because of that thought, she almost did it again. "Remember this guy was FBI at one point in his career, so he wasn't stupid." When Cain grunted, Celeste ignored the insult to the Bureau guys and continued.

"Every fast-food outlet within a hundred square miles turned over their security tapes. Not one man fitting Bremer's description ever came near one of their buildings that day.

"The autopsy also showed Bobby had been given a sleeping agent in his food before the barbital injection. Bremer would've shot him. Not loaded him with drugs before killing him. He had no reason to. A bullet is fast, simple. Military." She let her words sink in. "And Bremer wouldn't have taken the time to make sure Bobby's lucky coin was in his hand first."

"So you're telling me this other guy either did all of this to set you up—or he had a loving heart and killed Bobby in the least traumatic way possible."

"No, our killer doesn't have a heart or a conscious," she insisted, recalling that she'd made the exact same statement to Jonathon. "Bobby Cambridge's death was a foregone conclusion."

A knot of tension throbbed at the base of her neck— a nuisance she refused to give in to. "My being set up was a last-minute thought, triggered simply by my working the case—a case where this killer's client got cold feet and decided to take matters into his own hands. Otherwise, they would've have set me up with more than just one phone call on my cell. Either way, it was imperative the operation looked like a kidnapping."

That's what infuriated her the most, the wasted time, the useless words. The endless strategizing by the kidnap experts that had led them nowhere while Bobby's life slipped through their fingers like sand. "This guy was kind to Bobby just because that's his style. He meticulously researches his victims. Then he kills in the manner he decides fits the victim's profile. It's his trademark.

"Gabriel knew which Secret Service agent to seek out."

"Gabriel?"

"A nickname I gave him." She studied Cain in her peripheral vision and waited. The familiar feeling of inadequacy roiled within, but stubbornly she squelched it. She'd stand by her profile, no matter what Cain MacAlister thought.

"Okay," he drawled. "Let's say there was another player, someone who paid Bremer to kill Bobby. Why wouldn't this Gabriel turn it into a real kidnapping and take the money before he murdered the boy?" he prodded.

"Because Gabriel's a professional. Someone had already paid him for the job, most likely two or three times the ransom amount. He never wanted the president's money. Probably understood better than Bremer that the chances of seeing the money were infinitesimal. He needed a patsy to pull off the actual kidnapping."

Her mind raced through the details again. "He may even have masterminded the whole thing with very little input from Bremer. Just think, if Bremer hadn't died, right now he'd be the most wanted man alive—the man who murdered the president's ten-year-old son. There wouldn't have been a place on this planet he could hide. Gabriel couldn't afford to let him live. Bremer signed his own death sentence the moment he agreed to the kidnapping, he was just too arrogant to realize it."

"And since they believed that you were the accomplice, the FBI had no reason to look farther."

"The didn't have enough evidence against me and they had to let me go."

"Which is when, like Bremer, you became a liability once you were released."

"So the question is…who paid Gabriel?"

"And why?"

"If we find the who, we'll know the why."

Celeste noted Cain's *we* but didn't let it go to her head.

"So why the nickname Gabriel?"

"The angel coin." In her mind, it was a simple correlation. "I connected it to Gabriel the Archangel."

"The angel of mercy," Cain murmured. "If what you say is true, his motivation wasn't kindness."

"Still…" Celeste looked at Cain. "In his own twisted way, Gabriel kept Bobby away from the ugly."

"How ABOUT some food?" Celeste crossed the hardwood floor, her heels thudding her irritation with short, staccato beats. "My apartment is this way." Pointedly, she walked to the storeroom. "I have two entries, one from the store and another from a stairway at the side alley."

The stock room, a long, flat area that ran the width of the store, held very little merchandise. Mostly assorted lamps, a chest and two chairs, all with bright yellow tags marking them as layaway items.

"I don't believe in a lot of surplus."

A closet door, or so it seemed, graced the side wall. Beyond it lay a short flight of stairs that led to the second-floor apartment.

When they reached the top of the stair, she stabbed

a series of numbers into the security keypad. Once the alarm beeped, she opened the door.

Cain had expected an extension of the store. What he got was a surprise. The apartment was designed with a great room and a small hall that led to the two bedrooms and bath.

Simple. Uncluttered.

But then again, how cluttered can an apartment get when its furniture consisted of a Nautilus, free weights, sparring bag and treadmill?

A gymnasium, right down to the dull white walls and scuffed hardwood floor. She'd thrown in a brown corduroy sofa, threadbare on the arms and so mangled any decent flea market would have rejected it.

On the kitchen counter was a microwave and a portable television. A radio sat on the floor near the weights, filtering a sultry jazz throughout the room.

As long as Cain had known her, Diana had left music on twenty-four seven—for company, she used to joke.

But the scent that lingered was flowers and earth. Not roses and talcum. Because he could, he inhaled deeply. "Don't tell me—you're going for the featherweight championship this year," Cain mused.

"No, downstairs is home. This is my workspace."

"Still, I have to admit the right combination of chrome and iron does the heart good."

"Because Grams and I died, my inheritance went to several designated charities and everything that was Diana's stayed behind." A decision she'd made not realizing at the time the immense relief and freedom that had come with it.

"What happened to my mother's engagement ring, Gypsy?" The question slid out of nowhere. During her days of being interrogated, she'd learned those questions were the worst kind.

"I don't know," Celeste answered slowly, cautious of the minefield being laid. "After I left the letter breaking our engagement at your apartment, I forgot to leave it, too," she explained, feeling the lie as it slithered over her tongue and knowing the self-hatred that would follow. "It was lost when the car exploded. Flung from my hand most likely. It was never recovered."

"How did you survive the blast?"

Celeste closed her eyes, briefly, knowing he deserved an answer, but undecided on how much she deserved to hold back. "I'd been upset. Too upset to drive."

"Because of the investigation?"

"Yes, mostly. I'd only been released a few days before and still hadn't really recovered." Restless, Celeste went into the kitchen and turned on the water. "Grams talked me into spending some time with her. Do some shopping, maybe see a play. Just excuses to get away." After filling the kitchen basin, she slid in the few dirty dishes she'd left from lunch. "We were in your apartment parking garage. I had just dropped off my letter to you. I realized I'd forgotten to leave the ring, so I grabbed it from my purse and was going to run it upstairs. Grams insisted on driving."

Celeste smiled at the memory as she swiped the sponge over a sandwich plate, rinsed it and set it in the drainer. Even at seventy, her grandmother had refused to give into Father Time. "She'd wanted to get behind

the wheel of that Porsche ever since you'd given me the
car. I wasn't in any shape to drive and I had just enough
humor left to let her."

Nausea cramped her belly.

"Just that once," she whispered, knowing if she'd
said no, Grams might have survived. A bowl slipped
from her fingers and shattered on the floor. "Damn it!"

"Gypsy, it's not your—"

"Yes, it is." She spaced out the words, more to convince herself than him. "Don't you even dare think
about offering me sympathy. I don't want it."

She wanted to take her comment back, but the hard
planes of his face told her it was too late. Instead, she
grabbed the wastebasket beside the kitchen door.

"Anyway…" Kneeling by the counter, she began
tossing pieces of glass into the garbage. "I grabbed the
ring, threw my purse on the front seat and shut the door.
I hadn't taken more than one or two steps past the car
when she must have turned on the ignition."

Celeste sat on her heels and abandoned all pretenses
as the memories rushed back. "The explosion blew me
clear." She remembered the vicious body slam of heat.
"Grams screamed. I raised my head from the pavement
and saw her trying to get out, her hands…"

She shook her head trying to dislodge the sounds. "I
must have passed out. Jon told me that the heat was so
intense, it set a few more cars on fire. No one could get
close for a long time. Later they found me under a
pickup truck. Apartment Security records showed only
my signature. And since Grams' body was burned
beyond…" She cleared her throat, forcing the images

back. "The firefighters automatically assumed Grams was me. By the time they found me, I was covered in blood from a head wound. Before they figured out I was more than an innocent bystander at the wrong place at the wrong time, Jon had worked his government magic and I had died from the head trauma."

"How long were you in my apartment?"

"Grams and I were there a half an hour. No more. Just enough time to write the note and take my things." Ignoring the trembling of her fingers, she finished picking up the glass.

"Giving the killer plenty of time to rig the Porsche."

"He used the ignition to detonate the gas tank."

"Is that why you hesitated at the Jag this morning?

"Yes. It's also why I don't own a car." She shrugged. "Cars give me a bout of nausea. It usually passes in moments. A reaction from the explosion."

"It wasn't your fault, Gypsy."

She rose to her feet, furious with herself for letting her guard down, if only briefly.

"And Olivia?"

"She and Grams had been friends since Radcliff, remember? When Bobby disappeared, Olivia and I became quite close through the whole ordeal. She never believed I was involved."

By the time Celeste had snagged the broom from the pantry, swept up the splinters of the bowl and put it all away, Cain had set the last dish in the drainer to dry.

"I don't think I've ever seen you in the kitchen," she said, once they were finished. Unsettled, she tried to match this man to the one who'd been her fiancé. "Who are you?"

"I'm just a man, Celeste." He sat at the table and leaned back, watching her with hooded eyes. Lifting a shoulder negligently, he added. "Not much more to it."

There it was again, the detachment he'd shown when they'd dated. Only now, it plucked at her tightly strung nerves. Before, she'd just respected his privacy.

God, she'd been so naive.

"But there is," she argued, not quite putting her finger on the cause of her frustration.

His eyes captured hers, the gray in them smoky, the murky depths somehow reassuring. "Just ask me."

"I don't understand—"

"You can trust me." His tone dipped, touching off a sensitive chord somewhere deep within her. "That's what you want to know, isn't it?"

Automatically, she started to shake her head, only to stop in midmotion when she caught sight of his expression. Lord, he was arrogant. "Trust isn't just given." Nevertheless, something compelled her to do just that. She sat down and gripped her knees under the table. What was it about heroes that made you believe in them?

Heaven knew, she didn't want to.

"Gypsy," Cain covered her hand, his thumb stroking the soft pad of her palm. "How did Olivia discover you were alive?"

Aware the subject was no longer focused on Cain almost made her laugh. That had been the standard in their conversations. She'd ask a personal question, he'd deflect. Sometimes, it reminded her of a sparring match. One Cain always won. "I asked Jon to hold a funeral for Grams and me."

Celeste yanked her hand back, not wanting the sympathy the contact would bring. "God, it was awful. When my mother died, I was barely old enough to remember. I never thought…" She took a deep ragged breath, trying to dislodge the knot from her throat.

Born fatherless, Celeste had been dragged from city to city by a mother who'd been pampered all her life and followed any man who caught her mother's eye. At age five, Celeste's world had abruptly changed when her mother had died in a car wreck with another woman's husband. Within hours after her mother's death, Celeste had been placed in the care of her grandmother.

"I waited hours after everyone left, before I went to say my goodbyes." Petite, white-haired with a will made of tempered steel, Grace Taylor had once been a New York debutante. A loving, yet possessive woman, whose harsh ways had forced a daughter away. Once she'd gotten custody of Celeste, she'd refused to let her granddaughter repeat the past. She'd hired the best tutors and nannies, keeping Celeste always within reach. Secluded. "In spite of everything, I loved Grams.

"Olivia saw me at the cemetery. I didn't know she had a meeting with the cemetery director about our headstones. The man wanted to show her a statue near ours. You can guess the rest." Celeste smiled. "She almost fainted at my feet but recovered herself just in time to avoid giving my identity away to the director."

"The fact that Olivia's your friend doesn't absolve her from suspicion."

"I know. But this goes higher than her. Higher than you realize. We can't trust anyone."

"Including the president."

"Yes, especially him. Emotionally, Robert killing his son would be a leap. But logically..." Abruptly, she turned away, looking across the room, seeing nothing, Cain was sure. Her profile revealed the battle within. "God, why didn't Jon just take my secret to the grave?"

"Did you choose your alias or did Jon?"

"What?" Her head snapped back.

"You heard me."

"I don't have an *alias*."

In Cain's work, he'd used a hundred different identities through the years. Forgotten more than he remembered.

"Celeste Pavenic is who I am. Other than finding Bobby's murderer, my past doesn't exist."

"Everything from the past?" He saw her chin thrust forward, her eyes narrow. He would have been amused by her response, if he hadn't tuned into the fear behind the defiance. Been annoyed by it.

"Everything."

"I'm from your past." His statement hit the air with the heavy thud—a gauntlet thrown to the ground. And damned if he didn't want her to pick it up.

"Exactly."

The buzz of Cain's phone cut her off. "What is it?"

"Hey, boss."

"I'm nobody's boss," Cain replied, his harsh tone born from frustration with Diana more than from his brother Ian's flippancy.

"We both know Roman only accepted Mercer's position temporarily to give you time." Ian grunted. "But when you're running things, you might think about acquiring me before I change my mind and retire, too. This contracting thing could get old, you know."

It had only been a few weeks since Ian had resigned his naval commission, so Cain took the flippancy in stride. If his brother did anything outside of government work, it would be running their family business. The old man would love that, Cain thought, absently. It was a known fact that the youngest son of Quentin MacAlister had the gift for making great whiskey. "What do you have for me?"

"You were right about the car. Stolen last night from a couple on vacation. Rental."

"Okay, so what else you got?"

"There's been a rash of B and E's in your area."

"Burglaries? Go on."

"The police breakdown is on its way. Check your PDA. Looks like someone's been busy. There have been six break-ins in the last few weeks. Some businesses, mostly residential—all high-income targets. Nothing's surfaced on the street yet." There was a pause.

Cain heard Ian's fingers fly over his keyboard.

"In every case, they've used advanced tech equipment to gain access. Stuff only available to the upper echelons of the government." Ian's concern filtered over the phone. "I'm sending a list of projected targets with the report."

"Robberies?" Diana murmured the question.

Nodding, Cain grabbed the unit from his pocket. "Send the report, Ian."

After a short pause, his brother responded, "Here it comes. Notice the two topping the list."

As the data filled the screen, Cain zeroed in on the obvious.

"Olivia Cambridge," he noted. "The family mansion is located fifteen minutes from Shadow Point."

"She arrived at Shadow Point a few weeks back. Earlier than usual. Could be the auction but it's not her usual pattern." It was common knowledge the president's mother spent the colder months in Palm Beach. "I don't like it, Cain. My muse is talking." There was a pause. He let the words hang in the air. "The connection is too coincidental. And in my experience, an answer this clean usually stinks to high heaven by the time it's all over."

"Hell, it already smells," Cain added. "Mercer's shooting is tied in. I want that connection found, Ian. And while you're at it, get me more on Olivia Cambridge's charities, her bank accounts and who hangs out in her social circle here. There's a leak somewhere and Olivia Cambridge might lead us to it."

"Got it."

"And Ian…"

"What?"

"Be discreet. The president wouldn't be the first to sacrifice family for political gain. And I'm not so sure about his mother. Both are at the top of our list along with Vice President Bowden and the rest of the legislature. And until they're all cleared, we don't want anyone getting suspicious."

"Don't worry, brother. Discretion is my middle name." Ian's tone hardened over the possibility that the president might have killed his own son.

"How about the warehouse? What have you got on that?"

"I sent you the inventory. Looks like Mrs. Cambridge and her pals are storing some pretty pricey items for the charity auction."

"Get me the security schematics on the warehouse, the Cambridge estate and any other estates listed. Pull in favors if you have to."

"You'll have it by tonight. Roman's already working on it. He also said to watch yourself or there'll be hell to pay from Kate," Ian warned. "The pregnancy has left her hormonally challenged and this time he says you're on your own."

"I'll handle her if the need arises."

"What about Diana? How are you handling her?"

For some reason the question grated. "It's under control." But Cain's little voice was nudging him, laughing at his confidence.

"I see." The pause between the two words left no doubt what his little brother was thinking. Cain didn't bother correcting him. "She's there."

"Yes." It was a statement not a question, but Cain chose to answer anyway. "Anything else?"

Ian took the silent order to move on. "Yes." This time the pause was longer. "Lara's getting impatient."

"Only impatient?"

"If I didn't know you better, I'd think you find this situation amusing." Ian's sigh held a comical edge. "She doesn't like me keeping her in the dark like this, Cain. Hell, she just doesn't like me. Compound that with the fact that I'm stopping her from finding her father's killer—well, let's just say certain parts of my anatomy are at serious risk."

Cain almost smirked over the younger man's concern. Or the lack thereof. "You're tough, you can handle her," he responded, deliberately withholding sympathy.

"Hell, some things are just beyond the call of king and country. Since you trained her, you know she won't hesitate to maim me if she thinks I'm in her way. Which I am." Satisfaction rolled over the phone.

"Keep her pacified, Ian, but don't underestimate her. She was my best protégé," Cain ordered. "Right now, I don't have time to deal with a grief-stricken operative."

"Can I use brute force?"

Cain had recognized long ago that Ian was attracted to Jonathon Mercer's daughter. He wondered if his brother realized it yet. "Only if necessary. Lock her up if you have to. Just keep her out of my way. And call me with any updates." With that, Cain snapped the phone shut, not feeling the least bit bad about hanging up.

"Lara wants a crack at Jon's killer?"

"Yes, but I've enough to worry about, without having—"

A knock exploded through the room, making Diana jump. Quickly, she reached for her pistol then crossed to her apartment door. But before she could grab the knob, Cain was there, his hand flat against the wood.

"Ask who," he mouthed soundlessly.

"I was going to," she whispered harshly, her glare shifting to the trim black metal pistol he held—barrel up. "Who is it?"

"Jim Lassiter, Miss Pavenic." A throat cleared. "Can I have a moment of your time?"

Cain slipped the weapon back into his waistband and stepped partially into the room's shadows, his curiosity sparked by the unexpected visit. Understanding he might need the local law, Cain had run a background check on Sheriff Lassiter before arriving in Shadow Point.

He recalled that Lassiter, a widower in his late forties, had retired as a captain from the Detroit Police Department's Homicide Division. Two months prior, he had the accepted the position as the town's sheriff when no one local had anything even close to his qualifications.

After following suit with her weapon, Diana opened the door. "Hello, Sheriff." Her smile, Cain noted, was somewhat rigid, but her voice remained steady. "What can I do for you?"

"I'm sorry to disturb you, Miss Pavenic. But an hour ago, a drag race occurred on the road outside of town. I have a witness, a truck driver, who says one of the vehicle was a black Jaguar. It nearly ran his rig off the road." The sheriff pushed back the brim on his Stetson, uncovering a dark, receding hairline. "You were seen getting out of that same Jag here in town. Now, I have some pretty angry people wanting to get replacement on some damaged mailboxes."

"I understand—"

"Hello, Sheriff." Cain stepped beside her, opening the door wide to accommodate them both. "The car's mine." The hand Cain extended was grasped immediately. "I'm…Miss Pavenic's fiancé, Cain MacAlister. Sorry about the damage. I got carried away when some fool challenged me for my space on the road. When it got out of hand, I stopped my car, but the other car had already disappeared," Lassiter released Cain's hand. "I was going to report the incident but you beat me to it.

"Of course, I'll pay for the expenses." Cain removed his wallet from his pocket and handed the sheriff a business card. "Call that number and talk with my partner, Roman D'Amato, and he'll take care of everything."

After a glance at the card, Lassiter tucked it into his coat pocket. "Most of the folks will accept this. Others might not..." He shrugged. "Let's just say I know firsthand that some people aren't as amicable to strangers." He hooked his thumb through a front belt loop.

"If they don't accept it, have them contact me here. I'll take care of it." Casually, Cain slipped his arm over Diana's shoulder. "I'm hoping not to be categorized as a stranger around here for much longer. Isn't that right, sweetheart?"

"What?" Her gaze flickered, before she recovered, bestowing upon Cain a look of absolute adoration. "Oh, yes." She shifted her gaze to Lassiter. Her hand patted Cain's stomach, her fingers digging into its muscles as she snuggled deeper into his right side. Cain was sure the sheriff didn't notice. "I'm sorry, honey," she demurred with a laugh, before turning to Lassiter. "I'm still not used to the idea of being engaged."

"Well now, most folks didn't even know you were dating." Lassiter commented, his voice holding a hint of speculation.

"We met through mutual friends." She smiled. Still, Cain noticed the lines tighten at the sides of her mouth.

"I guess congratulations are in order." The sheriff's friendly manner didn't quite reach his eyes.

"Thank you. I'm a very lucky man, finding someone as special as…Celeste." Cain let his arm drop until his hand rested on the soft curve of her hip. He pinched her backside lightly. Immediately her fingers flexed, then relaxed against his stomach.

"Have you folks set a date?"

"Not yet," Cain answered first. "We're still working out the logistics with my family."

"MacAlister." The blue eyes studied Cain in a new light, his eyes drawn once again to the card. "As in MacAlister Whiskey?"

"Guilty," Cain acknowledged with practiced ease. "My father's company."

"I read about it in some financial magazine. Saw your picture." He grinned. "Caught my eye because it's my favorite brand."

"I'll tell my father you said so. He appreciates the feedback."

"You do that." Lassiter tipped his hat. "And since you're willing to provide restitution, I'll let you off with a warning. Call it an early wedding gift. Just see that it doesn't happen again."

"Thanks," Cain said, and slid his hand into the soft curls at the base of Diana's neck.

With her sharp intake of breath, Lassiter glanced up.

"Maybe you could come over some night for dinner," Cain suggested, keeping his tone casual.

The sheriff hesitated, then bobbed his head until his chin disappeared into the thick collar of his coat. "I'd like that. Hell, I'm getting tired of diner food—" He tipped his hat low onto his forehead. "Excuse me, Miss Pavenic."

Lassiter extended his hand once more to Cain. "Congratulations again on your engagement."

"Thank you, Sheriff."

Cain watched the other man leave before shutting the door.

"You can stop now," she snapped and tried to sidestep his hold.

"I could," he stated, refusing to drop his arm. "I'm just not sure I want to." He pulled her body closer, noting when the heavy lashes that shadowed her cheeks flew up in surprise.

"Gypsy." He drew out her nickname, enjoying the taste of it against his tongue. Sweet, he thought, too damn sweet to handle the bitterness in him. Nonetheless, he cupped the back of her neck, urging her closer. He noted a small flicker of alarm, right before her eyes deepened into cerulean pools. He gentled his touch, no longer surprised over his concern for her.

Unable to stop himself—not wanting to stop himself—Cain studied her clean-scrubbed features, following the graceful line of her face until his gaze rested on the slightly moist tendrils of hair that clung to her forehead and cheeks.

"Consider this…" he challenged softly, enjoying the minklike texture of her hair against his skin. He leaned in, allowing his mouth to hover above hers. "Redefining the term *we*."

Chapter Seven

The kiss itself was gentle. Only a butterfly dusting against her lips. Still, Celeste's heart trembled.

"What are you doing?" Her voice, rough, blended with the muffled roar cresting in her ears. But it was the fire in his eyes that set her trembling. His voice dipped seductively, strumming a chord deep within her long and hard, until her toes curled.

"Satisfying your curiosity." The warmth of his breath tickled, then excited. "And mine. Isn't that what you wanted?" Sparks of electricity raced up her arm, leaving her skin tingling. When his thumb rubbed the pad of her hand lightly, she couldn't control her sharp intake of breath.

"Pretending we're a couple…" The impulse to bury his fingers in the damp curls, to draw her face up to his, increased the hammering in Cain's blood. He struggled to keep his expression bland. "…simplifies things."

"Simplifies—" The word came out in a squeak. She cleared her throat, obviously trying to gain some control over her anger. The action drew his gaze to the small, erratic pulse at the base of her neck increasing his craving for that spot—sweet and fragile—under his mouth. "Can't you be honest with me for once?"

"You first."

When Cain's gaze caught and pinned hers, any thought Celeste had of fighting disappeared under a surge of longing. His free hand skimmed her jaw before slipping around to cup the back of her head. The small hairs on her neck stood.

"You want honesty?" He leaned closer until his breath tickled her cheek. Without a thought, Celeste shifted her mouth to taste the warmth on her lips and he captured her in a slow, shivery kiss. There was a cautious intimacy in the way his lips caressed hers. The kiss spanned three years of yearning, of deprivation that started in her heart and grew until it overwhelmed her soul, leaving her body throbbing.

"This is honest, Gypsy," he whispered after his mouth broke away. He nibbled her lower lip, the curve of her jaw.

"No," she disagreed, but in spite of herself, Celeste waited, her breath locked in her throat, the anticipation making her heart race. "It's a weapon."

Cain absorbed the insult, accepting the lie for what it was—an act of self-preservation. He stroked the soft skin of her neck with the tip of his finger. Her lips trembled and Cain's blood raced. Enough that when her lips parted as if to say something more, he moved closer. The slight switch in positions fanned his desire, touching off a high-pitched hum throughout his body.

Shock rippled over her features, telling him she felt it, too. But the fear remained in the widening of her eyes.

His body tightened, every muscle rigid with aware-ness. The attraction was there—flash-fire hot. After ev-erything she'd been through, everything she'd done, she still wanted him. He'd bet his sanity on it.

"Stop it!" Her words exploded between them, a little breathless, more than a little desperate. Taking a deep, unsteady breath, she stepped back, startled when Cain's hand fell away. He let her go, using the time to bank his desire, to silence the hum.

"I have no idea what game you're playing." Her hands went to her hips, though a charming flush invaded her cheeks. "But I'm not interested."

"This isn't a game, Gypsy." Regret, finely edged and razor-sharp, sliced through him. "And you *are* inter-ested. But I agree, this situation is complicated enough." When she didn't respond, he wasn't surprised.

For a moment, Celeste hadn't thought it'd be so easy. And for a moment, she didn't want it to be.

"I want guarantees," she insisted, albeit weakly.

"Go ahead," he folded his arms, evidently uncon-cerned and more annoyingly, unaffected.

"Don't think I'm going to be like Lassiter." Celeste glared. "He used your father's reputation to size you up. Right about now, he's wondering how I met you for real and how long you'll be staying."

"You're going to have to trust me on this," he ordered. "And not go off half-cocked."

As usual, his features remained impassive. She'd spent her life on the fringe of society. Over the years, she'd learned to observe, to read people from their actions, voice inflections, facial expressions. But she'd never been able to read Cain MacAlister. "I'm not the one in this room who's the self-appointed protector of mankind, Prometheus."

"We're not talking about me."

"Good thing, because we could definitely talk about some control issues, couldn't we?"

Cain sighed. "Why don't we stick to the reason we're here."

"Fine." On stilted legs, Celeste led him to her second bedroom. The smell of fresh paint lingered in the air as they entered, a by-product of the pristine white walls.

"So tell me more about this killer," Cain said.

"Personality wise?" She switched on a nearby lamp. "Detached. Unaffected."

"Your typical antisocial type?" Cain's eyes narrowed against the low amber light filtering the room.

"Actually, he's extremely sociable and very comfortable moving around in elite circles." When Cain stepped behind her, the room seemed to close in on Celeste. She flipped on additional lights, hoping to widen the space. "Otherwise, he wouldn't have access to the people he's targeting."

"Okay, so how did you hook him?" In one long sweep, Cain's gaze took in her office. Or what she'd always thought of as her office.

"A few months ago, the killer left the first series of coins."

"First series? How many all together?"

"Including Jonathon's, four."

"Nothing showed up because—"

"At my request, Jonathon made sure it didn't."

"I believe you're beginning to impress me, Gypsy." His gaze skimmed over the wallpaper—only it wasn't paper, but photographs—that covered one wall. Some were of Bobby, some were of his family and other Shadow Point residents. Others were of people who were no longer alive—their few smiling portraits framed by pictures of their corpses—some were riddled with blood and gore, others not. Spattered atop and in between lay a rainbow of Post-it notes. At one time, these people had been strangers to Celeste, but not anymore. Over the last few months, she'd become intimately familiar with these individuals and their backgrounds.

Cain let out a low, easy whistle. "If anyone but me saw this, they might think you were a serial killer. Or at the very least, a very sick individual."

She had to agree. Other than the photos, the room held little more than a cheap particle-board desk, a swivel chair and a computer. Somehow, she couldn't bring the coziness of her store into something that contained such evil. He scanned the photographs. "You're sure this is a man?"

"I'm sure. Men posture differently, physically as well as mentally. I'd say we're looking for a Caucasian male in his prime. Somewhere in his forties. Any younger would make it difficult for him to mingle with that kind of crowd. Any outstanding features, like a mole or scar would've been surgically removed. No habitual behavior. Easier to switch identities that way."

Cain grabbed his cell phone from his pocket and punched in a number. With a decisive "Call me," Cain snapped the phone shut.

"Money, his reputation, that's what drives him." She glanced at the pictures on the wall until she came to Bobby's. "How he kills, that's just…a diversion." She smoothed her hand over the photograph, absorbing the familiar ache. "Mercer believed me from the beginning, but with no proof, he wasn't going to take it to the president. We'd already decided to continue investigating. My death made it easier."

"And Olivia Cambridge?"

"After she spotted me at the cemetery she contacted Jon and insisted I move to Shadow Point or she'd blow my cover. She knew I'd continue the investigation and wanted firsthand knowledge.

"Jonathon took a risk and I stayed here to make my dealing with her easier."

Cain nodded, but continued to scrutinize the other photos. "And Jonathon kept your presence here in Shadow Point a secret."

"Yes."

"President Cambridge wouldn't have been the first leader in history to kill a family member to ensure his position. Sympathy goes a long way with the American public during election years. However, when I suggested the theory to Jonathon, he didn't agree. If his death is connected to these others, you can be sure it's a paid contract. I just don't know who the client is or the why."

"He can't kill all of us," Cain argued.

"That's my point. He could if he wanted to. I'm betting whoever is paying him has found an access to all of our files."

"A government official?"

Celeste nodded. "Or another operative." The Labyrinth files were classified. Even the president had restricted access unless he required contact.

"Jon wouldn't allow the records—"

"And as you've pointed out before, Cain, Jonathon's dead. Besides, this guy doesn't waste his time. He wouldn't be playing with the coins if he wasn't already getting paid to kill these people," she replied. "He's meticulous—pays enormous attention to detail. Everybody knew Jonathon always stepped outside alone to smoke his cigars.

"I'm betting that the coins started showing up because he'd realized I survived the explosion." Edgy, Celeste opened a small fridge under her desk and grabbed a bottle of water. Absently she offered it to Cain, but he shook his head. "If I had to speculate on the two highest probabilities…" She pointed the bottle in the general direction of the photos. "…when he tries to kill us, he's going to do it in such a way that he'll show off his skill, his cunning, or he'll set us up for another murder."

"Or both."

"That, too," she admitted easily. "Cain," she warned, "don't underestimate this guy. His reputation is everything. He doesn't make mistakes. In his business, if he did, he'd be dead."

"You forget, I'm in the same business."

"I haven't forgotten." She started past him, but his arm came up to block her retreat. For an instant, she thought the muscle flexing against her breast might have been deliberate.

"Still enemies?" His eyes slid over her face, questioning. But it was the purr behind the words that stroked her heart, set its tempo faster.

"Uncomfortable allies," she tossed back. Heavens, she'd never trusted anyone except Grams before Cain. Never really understood that trust took on a different meaning when dealing with passion—or love for that matter. Not that she had a lot of experience with either.

Oh, she'd had the typical clichéd affair with one of her professors in college. Not because she'd found true love, but more because she thought herself sophisticated enough to deal with sex. But when that professor found another willing student to add to the notches on his bedpost, she bowed out gracefully, not caring, but not liking the bad taste the situation had left in her mouth.

From that moment, she'd avoided any kind of involvement…until Cain. He released inhibitions in her that she'd never known existed and a love she never thought herself capable of.

So now, when desire sharpened his granite-like features, a succession of small electric charges exploded at the base of her spine.

In another place, another lifetime, Cain could've been the lover she desired, the husband she dreamed about. "Cain, I—" Celeste stopped, not knowing what to say.

"It's all right, Gypsy." He dropped his arm, turned toward the photos once more. "So Gabriel works alone?"

With a bit more steadiness than she was feeling, Celeste swung away, not sure what to think of the abrupt change in Cain. How could someone turn off emotion so quickly? Especially when her own roiled within.

"For the most part—yes. Partners are dangerous, unreliable," she said, setting her bottled water onto the desk. Water would only aggravate her already fluttering stomach. "Gabriel tracks his victim's life, learns their habits then kills them. Obviously, he decided we're important enough to study."

"So, like you, he profiles people."

"Yes, to put it simply."

"And the coins are just his way of keeping our attention."

Celeste rubbed her temples tiredly. "The coins appeared a couple of months ago—on the body of a man by the name of Doctor Alejandro Longoria."

"Spanish." Cain took a moment to place the name. "Expert in plastic surgery. Spoke at a seminar here in the States just before he died. Interpol suspected he'd been killed by an unsatisfied customer."

"He was. I believe one of his patients, possibly a surgery gone wrong, hired Gabriel to kill Longoria."

"His face was shredded—his heart cut out. All with his own scalpel."

"And all the facial incisions were precise, as though the killer had been following a map or—"

"Copying the same incisions made on his disgruntled customer."

"Five Georgia quarters were found in his coat," Celeste explained. "Their emblem consisted of a peach, an oak tree and a banner with three words. Wisdom. Justice. Moderation. The authorities didn't think it unusual because Dr. Longoria was known to be collecting them from Americans who passed his way."

"But you disagree."

"Do you remember when Supreme Court Justice Miles Rokeach died?"

Cain grunted, disgusted. "Someone breached his yacht, most likely from under the water. Easy enough. Pay off a crew member, arrange for a predetermined location, then kill the contact with the rest of the crew. The authorities didn't find the ship for several days and the crew members were gone. Most likely thrown overboard."

"The authorities found Justice Rokeach and his wife dead inside."

"And you believe your assassin left the Georgia quarters in Longoria's coat as a clue," Cain prompted, unwilling to use kid gloves on Celeste. "That's pretty vague. So far the only connection is the word *justice*."

"And the southern state of Georgia," she countered, obviously not intimidated. "Don't you see? After rendering them unconscious with a stun gun, the killer stripped them naked and sealed them in the cabin. But not before he'd left a canister of hydrogen cyanide gas behind. He rigged a timer to allow both of them to regain consciousness before the canister detonated. They were found dead by the door."

"I heard the rumors. A white supremacy group backed the murders in protest over the judge's religion. He was Jewish."

"Exactly. And in their nightstand ashtray lay five state quarters. New Hampshire. The Old Man on the Mountain."

"Mercer?"

"The president had nicknamed Jonathon Old Man."

"Again you're stretching, Gypsy."

"And he's dead."

Celeste caught Cain's gaze. "I've tracked Gabriel back four years. Men, women, children. Diplomats, mob figures, the cartel. I can't be one-hundred-percent positive, but all were hired hits, all were killed with Gabriel's flair. None with coins until after Bobby's death."

"Why the coins? And why now? Because of your report on the coin left in Bobby's hand?"

"It fits. Otherwise, why not a note, a memento, like jewelry or a flower?"

"It's all been done before."

"Exactly. Not original enough."

"Speaking of jewelry, Gypsy…" Cain paused, watching her face. "How about telling me the truth about my mother's engagement ring?"

"I told you—"

"No more lies. I realized when Jon told me you were alive that you might have kept it. You see, I placed a homing device in it with a fifty-mile range so when I tried to find you I turned it on. I got no response. Not until this morning, that is."

"That's how you found me so quickly at the lighthouse." She took a deep breath. "You actually kept track of me with a homing device."

"No, it was a precaution. One I never used."

"I guess we've both lied, haven't we?"

At some point Cain had become important to her again. The actual moment it had happened didn't matter. It disturbed her more that he had.

"I guess we have."

Deep down, she realized she had even started hoping

that she'd found something with him again. Something special. But how could that hope survive when she disagreed with everything he stood for—or expected.

"This isn't going to work." Not the mission, not the relationship, she thought. She'd figure out another way to trap Gabriel. She bit her lip to keep it from trembling. No one besides Grams had ever cared enough to protect her. But Celeste didn't fool herself. Where Grams protected out of love, Cain did it out of duty.

Unfortunately, Celeste wanted—needed—love. Not protection.

Cain caught her by the elbow. She closed her eyes, resisting the temptation to turn into the comfort of his arms. How pathetic could she be?

"Leave me alone, Cain." Her lids fluttered open, unable to hide the entreaty.

"No. You've been alone too long already."

"Stop playing Freud." She bit back the urge to kick him in the shins. "What are you going to do when this is over? If we aren't dead that is."

"I'll leave." His answer was gruff. "Because it's for the best."

When she thought she couldn't care any more, hurt any more, his confession proved her wrong. "Whose best?"

"In the past, I might have protected you the wrong way. And I'm sorry for that. But I did it for the right reasons. Left with the same situation, I'd do it again. And while I'm here, no one is going to hurt you. Not Gabriel. Not his client. No one. I'll make sure of that."

And who is going to protect me from you? she wondered silently, already knowing the answer. The answer didn't matter because she understood that it was already too late. When Cain left, he'd be taking a part of her with him.

"Come on." He hugged her to his side. "I'm still hungry."

Celeste snuggled deeper under his arm, understanding what was beneath the words—what he hadn't said. He cared for her. "Are you suggesting that I feed you?" she asked, not in the mood to deal with her rioting emotions.

"No. I'm telling you to."

Even though his expression hadn't changed, Celeste knew he was joking. She wasn't in any mood for that either. "Then you'd better ask nicely or so help me—"

"Please?"

The shock of that one softly spoken word smacked the breath from her lungs. But it was the smile that came with it that almost brought her to her knees.

"I've got vegetable soup," she whispered, forcing her feet to keep her balanced. "Canned."

She'd forgotten how blatantly sexual his smile could be. The flash of white teeth, the slight tilt of his lips that hinted at some unknown male secret.

He leaned down and kissed her, catching her gasp of surprise with his mouth. Laughing, he did it again before using his free hand to guide her through the doorway. "You remembered my second weakness."

She looked up at him, fighting the desire to touch the dark stubble on his jaw, to kiss the hard line of his lips— lose herself in the strength of both. Quick to tease. Tender. Romantic. This had been the man she'd known.

The one who'd swept her off her feet, discovered her passion. It was the other part of him, Prometheus, who had broken her heart. "Cain—"

"No more questions for now." He touched his finger to her lips, then inhaled sharply when she kissed it. "First we'll eat, then we'll worry."

"Not so fast," she mused, knowing he did it deliberately. Dangled that carrot. "What's your first weakness?"

His hand drifted up to caress the nape of her neck.

"Obstinate gypsies."

THE DINNER was relatively easy. Cain ended up fixing it while Celeste took a shower.

Dressed in a light blue turtleneck sweater and jeans, she sat down with him and ate a grilled cheese sandwich and canned vegetable soup. Two cans, Celeste corrected, since Cain wasn't satisfied with one bowl.

"You're not cut out for this job, Celeste." Cain leaned back, and wiped his mouth with a napkin. "You should be teaching or raising a family."

"That's funny coming from you."

Cain stiffened ever so slightly, enough for Celeste to realize how harsh she'd sounded. When he stood, she caught his hand, gave him a small squeeze. "I'm sorry. I didn't mean that."

Before he could answer, the radio switched songs, catching Celeste's attention. "Hear that?" she asked. The radio played a familiar Nat King Cole melody.

Cain nodded.

"It was one of Grams' favorites," she whispered, not wanting to ruin the peacefulness of the moment.

"You miss her terribly, don't you?" He whispered, too, but the words came out rough, whiskey-soaked.

There'd been a time when passion had deepened his words, not sympathy.

"Yes. But I've missed you more."

For a moment, time slowed. His hands slipped up her arms bringing her closer. "For what it's worth, Gypsy, I've missed you, too."

His gaze caught her, now silver pools of molten diamonds. It was too easy to get lost in the way he looked at her—in the way he made her feel.

Shifting, he backed her up to the wall. The cold pine went unnoticed as the heat of his body eased between her legs.

"Please, I don't want…" Not when she felt this raw, this vulnerable. She shook her head, unable to finish.

"That's the problem." He caught her chin with the tip of his finger. The muscles quivered just under her jaw, but this time it wasn't from fury. "I do."

Chapter Eight

Cain braced his forearms against the wall on either side of her head and sank deeper into the embrace, using only his hips to force her flush against the wall. His mouth dropped to her ear, grazing the delicate curve of her lobe. A sharp nip, a light stroke of his lips turned the quivers into a violent flux of tremors.

Desperate, Celeste turned her head away, realizing her mistake instantly. He swooped to nuzzle her neck. His warm, damp breath raised goose bumps everywhere his lips skimmed. She wedged her hands between them but instead of pushing, they held on as memories stirred.

"Cain." His name came out quick, riding another gasp of pleasure. "I'm afraid."

"Ah, Gypsy." His hand slipped under her sweater and around to her back, tracing small, lazy circles at the base of her spine.

His fingers should've been icy, but they weren't. Hot flames of desire licked at her skin wherever he touched.

"I'm the last person you should be afraid of."

The warmth of his palm cupped the curve of her

waist. His thumb brushed gently against the small in-dentation just above her hip. A thick, liquid heat flowed, forming a whirlpool low in her belly. With a moan she arched, grinding against him, trying to ease the sensation.

Somewhere in the distance, she heard a slight buzzing. It took her a second to recognize the gentle slide of her jeans zipper. Instinctively, she gripped his wrist.

Turning her hand, he pressed a kiss to her palm. His tongue darted out to trace a delicate crease. A groan escaped her. His nostrils flared at the sound, but it was his gaze that changed her mind. The gray irises had sharpened to silver lightning, telling her exactly what he wanted.

A sense of urgency drove her. She couldn't have stopped her response, even if she'd wanted to.

And it pleased him. Very much, she realized. There was that maddening air of arrogance surrounding him again, but this time it seduced her.

Slowly, his hand slipped under her sweater again, this time lifting it, exposing her to his gaze. A flutter rose through her chest, swelled in her throat. His hand slid across her taut belly, his fingers icy but his palm fiery hot. Her breath caught with the snap of her bra's front clasp.

"Beautiful," he murmured. He eased the cup of her bra aside and gently outlined her breast with his fingertips, tracing the curves with infinite care. The caress spiked the currents of desire already racing through her. Her breasts swelled and she shifted closer, hoping the erotic strokes of his fingers would ease their ache.

His knuckles brushed the ring hanging from her neck, sending it skittering across her breastbone. She gasped. Her eyes met his and the possessive heat in them made her tremble.

"I'm glad you kept my ring," he whispered.

But when he drew away, Celeste heard a whimper, surprised that it had come from her.

"Hold on," he coaxed, the seduction melting over her like warm butter. He flipped her around so that her stomach pressed the wall, his pelvis bumped against the crevice between her buttocks. When she groaned, he pushed again, straining. The intensity ripped through her, savage. "When we were on the rope…" He pulled down the neck of her sweater, just enough to graze his teeth down the side of her neck. "I wanted…needed to do this."

"Yes." With slow deliberation, she rubbed, eliciting a hiss against her ear. "Me, too."

Slowly, he turned her back, lifting her legs up around his hips, his mouth slanting over hers, fusing their passion, blurring her thoughts.

"More," he demanded, his voice raw, his body rigid. He guided her hand under his sweater. "All."

Hair, thick and coarse, tickled her palm. A delicious shudder heated her body, causing her fingers to curl, her throat to hum.

His muscles quivered then bunched beneath her touch. His heart skipped a beat. Power surged through her. The hum she held escaped in a satisfied purr.

Tentatively, she moved her fingers, this time brushing her nails lightly across his chest, remembering with deliberate slowness his pleasure points. She smiled when a long, deep groan rasped against her ear.

His thumb brushed the hard peak of her breast.

But it wasn't enough. Unable to use words, she pulled at his shoulders, trying to bring him closer. Still, his touch was light, painfully teasing and totally in control.

A moan of frustrated pleasure slipped past her slightly parted lips. His mouth covered hers, this time dominating more than persuading. Her emotions whirled and skidded. She grabbed his hair, holding him, holding on, mindless to everything except the edge of desperation that crept between them.

Cain broke away, his hand fisted in her hair, his teeth at her neck, feasting. "Diana—"

Celeste froze.

"Stop!" She pushed away, her hands hitting his chest, demanding release. Nausea whiplashed through her. "Stop it, you bastard!"

Abruptly, Cain released her only to grab her arm when she started to fall. "Damn it! You're making it sound like I just betrayed you by whispering another woman's name. You *are* Diana!"

"No, I'm not!" The tears were there, swelling before she could blink them away.

"From where I stand, lady..." he ground out the words as his gaze raked her body. "You most definitely are."

Once again, Celeste found herself hauled closer, held by both shoulders, her eyelashes almost brushing his. It was beginning to be a habit with Cain, she thought angrily, then stopped. Shock rippled through her.

The lighthouse, the car and now. All three times he'd grabbed her in anger. No kid gloves. No fragile care. Cain would never have done that three years ago. He'd never grabbed Diana like that. Always in control, always even-tempered.

Angry, irritated…even in the midst of passion, Cain always maintained control.

It was a sobering thought. She'd been just as guilty as he about comparing now to the past.

"Cain, I'm—"

"So am I, *Diana*." Slowly, he let her slide until her feet touched the floor. "So am I." He turned away, the disgust underlining his movement. "I'm going to sleep on the couch. Tomorrow, we'll check out Olivia Cambridge."

Celeste didn't argue, understanding by his rigid stance that he was beyond listening. Maybe even beyond caring.

Still, for a split second, if he had lifted his arms she would've fallen into them, placed his heart beneath her cheek and wept.

Another sobering thought.

Silently, she walked to her room and quietly closed the door.

Chapter Nine

Detroit, Midnight

The wind whipped icy shards of snow and bits of garbage across the deserted pavement of Michigan Avenue. Only the neon lights of the strip clubs and adult bookstores revealed signs of life as they glowed like dim beacons above the heads of a few prostitutes huddled in doorways. Obviously, it was easier to freeze to death than to face their pimps with empty pockets.

Gabriel eased the dark green sedan to a stop in front of a triple-X theater where a lone hooker guarded her territory. The marquee cast a jaundiced glow over the entrance, accenting the woman's sunken eyes, the hollowness of her cheeks.

She'd been talking on her cell phone when she caught sight of his car. Quickly, she finished the conversation and placed her phone in the small beaded purse hanging at her side.

Come here, the man urged silently. He pressed a button to lower the tinted window on the passenger side. A blast of frigid air rifled through the interior, but he enjoyed the sensation. The ride into the city had been long and stuffy.

After darting a glance up and down the street, the prostitute brushed her blond bangs away from her forehead— only to have her fingers snag in the uncombed strands.

He waved to her and fought a sting of impatience when the woman hesitated, wobbling slightly on her stiletto heels. His hands tightened over the steering wheel when indecision crossed her face.

After a moment, she straightened and took several shaky steps forward. Her bare legs, protected from the elements by only a purple micro-mini, drew his attention. Even in the darkness, he noted the deep bruising around her feet and ankles. Confident there'd be track lines by the marks, he relaxed his hands.

She stuck her head through the open window and gripped the edge of the car with trembling fingers. The smeared mascara around her bloodshot eyes gave her a ghoulish look. "Hey, baby, wanna party?"

Up close, he noticed the harsh creases set in the planes of her face and estimated her age at around thirty. This line of work tended to age women rapidly, so admittedly, he could be off by five years or more. But the pale, almost translucent skin told him that the slight twitching of her shoulders and arms wasn't from the cold weather. This woman had already had her fix for the evening.

"I'd enjoy a party," he murmured and unlocked the car.

She slid into the seat and immediately the distinct scent of wet dog and stale cigarettes permeated the air.

Not bothering to tug her skirt back into place, she provided him with a glimpse of her merchandise as he pulled away from the curb.

He felt, rather than saw, her glance over his suit. "Are you a cop?" Her voice was husky, reminding him of Janis Joplin.

He allowed his lips to form a cultured smile. "No, just a businessman."

"Hmm." Seeming satisfied, she relaxed against the upholstered seat. "Well, businessman, I get a hundred bucks an hour for straight sex. Anything fancy or weird boosts the rate to three hundred." She looked at his leather gloves as he turned the steering wheel. "I'm not into pain, so no whips or handcuffs."

The light at Woodward Avenue turned red and the driver stopped. "How about…" he drawled, before letting his gaze move suggestively over her emaciated body. "…I pay you in crack."

Greed flickered across the pinpoint pupils of her glazed blue eyes. "Now you're talking, honey." She leaned into him, letting her hand drift over the zipper of his pants while her tongue licked the thick red gloss covering her upper lip. "Or you could pay me in cash and we share the groceries."

"Better yet, I'll show you a drug that will take you flying and we don't party at all." Gabriel slipped his hand behind her neck and pricked the skin under her ear with a small needle.

Surprise, then fear flitted across her face before she fell unconscious against his shoulder.

With little effort, he shoved her back onto the passenger seat. The small drug dose, combined with the other substances in her body, would be enough to kill her soon enough.

After turning south on Woodward, he checked his rear mirror, satisfied when no car appeared behind them. He pulled to the curb, cut the engine and lights before reaching for the woman's purse and snagging her cell phone. Careful not to put his mouth too close to the receiver, the man punched in a number.

"Hello." The male voice was hoarse from sleep.

"I received your request," the man stated, casually studying the snowflakes landing on the windshield. "So talk."

"How did you get this number?" The tone was enraged, all traces of sleep gone. "Only my family has access to my private line."

"That's not important. What's important is that you broke our agreement. You weren't to contact me so soon." Flicking a glance at the unconscious woman, he added. "Your message proved inconvenient."

"It couldn't be helped. I hired you to do a job. One that may be in jeopardy." His client took an agitated breath. "With the news of Jonathon Mercer's death, the security assigned for our target has been restructured."

The man relaxed. "There was always that possibility. The government tends to get jumpy when one of their own is killed."

"I want you to be prepared. Nothing can go wrong." His client's agitation grew with the demand.

"I've agreed to the job, I'll make the hit. There'll be no interference."

"Just make sure of it. There's too much at stake."

"So you have said, many times." Indifferently, the man leaned over and checked the woman's pupils, then her pulse. "By the way, my fee has doubled."

"Doubled? After you screwed up with the woman, I don't—"

"Celeste Pavenic is a minor…hiccup. She'll be taken care of when I'm ready, not before. As you said, added security means a greater chance of discovery. Hence, a need for larger risks. If you don't like it, find someone else." He started to hang up.

"All right. You'll get your money."

"I'm sorry, I didn't hear you," he replied and slapped the prostitute's face. There was no reaction.

"I said, you'll get your money."

"Then I agree." The man shifted back into his seat. "You'll do as before. Deposit the payment to the same account. Half now, the rest when the news hits the wire."

"It'll be done tomorrow."

And moments after the deposit, the money would be transferred through several different accounts until it reached the correct one overseas. "Do not inconvenience me again." Sharp steel edged each word. "Or the deal's off. Understood?"

"Yes. Yes," the other man replied, his drawl growing thicker with his impatience. "There will be no more contact between us. Just take care of business. You understand?"

The man in the car disconnected, tempted to take the imbecile's money and not do the job. He drove along the Detroit River until he found an acceptable area. The snow and wind sharpened off the water. The long, bellowing gusts had left the road deserted. He leaned over the woman and pushed the door open. Not bothering to get out, he shoved her onto the roadside and watched her roll a few feet. "*Au revoir, chérie,*" he said, as he tossed the purse out. Seconds later, his calling cards followed. He watched the silver glint against the snow, then reached for the camera in the glove compartment. "Say cheese," he quipped, then pressed the button.

As he closed the door, he replayed the telephone conversation in his mind, then spoke aloud as though the man on the other end were sitting beside him. "Tomorrow afternoon, my friend, you will learn of the dead prostitute. What I wonder is how you will explain the presence of your private number on her cell phone?" He settled against the leather seat for the long trip home. "Now *that* will be inconvenient."

CAIN LAY on the couch, understanding immediately when the worn cushions gave way—comfortable, comforting—why the piece had avoided the garbage dump.

But soon her scent clouded around him. He'd done his best to ignore it after she'd stepped out of the shower, smelling as if she'd rolled in a meadow of wild flowers.

Another change. Diana had been upper Manhattan, her scent more stylish, classy and serene. Restless, he stood and watched Pan pad out the kitchen door, most likely to start his nightly prowl. Cain soon started stalking the apartment himself. Checking windows, doors.

He caught sight of the weight bench and automatically loaded up the bar, although he was impressed at the sixty pounds she'd left there. Celeste Pavenic was as far from Diana as Manhattan was from the Rocky Mountains. Earthy, simple—strong. Although not as Rambo-strong as she thought she was.

Rhythmically, he lifted the weights. Damned if she wasn't impressing him. Scaring the hell out of him, too.

Cain had vehemently argued with Jon over her acquisition into Labyrinth. She'd been too raw, too delicate to survive out in the field.

But there was more to it. At Quantico, Jon and Cain had observed Diana through a two-way mirror. Dressed in a trim, navy-blue suit with a skirt just high enough to show a little too much thigh, and hair long enough to keep her femininity intact, she could've been a corporate poster girl.

But surprisingly, it was the air of efficiency that drew his attention. She leaned over a desk, her hand resting lightly on the shoulder of a redheaded man whose face was nothing more than an explosion of freckles. They both scanned the computer screen in front of them, pointing at data, deep in conversation.

Then, almost as if she sensed their presence, her head tilted just enough to study the mirror. The man continued to talk while she continued to stare. After a moment, she smiled, a soft serene tilt of her lips, before allowing her associate to pull her attention back to their discussion.

The impact of that one look, calm as a glass-covered pond, settled the frenzied storm in Cain. He'd spent years dealing with scum, mucking around in places where only the foulest creatures bred.

She'd became his beacon, an oasis amidst the chaos.

His decision to seduce her came at that moment, however, it had taken months for him to arrange the meeting through Roman. Then, for four months he'd courted her, leaving his seduction until the end.

She'd surprised him. In Cain's mind, gypsies had always been tall and sultry. After one weekend in his cabin, she had shattered that image forever. The memory of her sighs, soft and fluttering with uncertainty, still haunted him—how her heart had raced with each caress, how her moans of erotic pleasure had turned into demands for release. And when he hadn't obeyed right away, how she'd risen to meet him, naked and passionate, her skin slick with heat, her body pliant—her heart open.

Then he'd proposed.

He'd offered her passion, comfort, protection—if not love. And when she'd needed the protection, the comfort…he'd had no choice about leaving her. Another operative, Jordan Beck, had been captured and left to die in the bowels of Colombia. Cain had been his only line out.

As a satellite operative, Diana should never had been in real danger, the interrogation should've been routine.

But she'd stuck to her theory after the boy's death. Not once had she broken under the endless grilling.

For days, they'd kept her at a table, pounding her with questions. But while her answers never changed, Diana did. Her voice hoarsened to sandpaper, her features sharpened and her cheeks hollowed. Given little sleep and even less food, she'd taken it all with dignified grace, defying their allegations. All the while, he was sure, silently grieving for the dead boy.

Guilt twisted his gut because even knowing what he did now, he would have made the same choice.

"Cain."

She'd whispered his name from across the room, but the underlining desperation smacked him square in the gut.

Slowly, he set down the weights.

She'd changed her clothes. A man's plain white T-shirt hung to her knees over a dark pair of sweatpants and fleece scuffs on her feet for added warmth. No makeup, her hair in feathered disarray, she looked more like a teenager than a grown woman.

"I know its not fair for me to ask this, but…" She stopped in mid-step, poised to turn and run. "Oh, hell."

Cain had been around her enough now to realize she only swore when she felt cornered or off balance.

But he wasn't paying attention to the words, as much as to the need reflected in her eyes. Not desire, but reassurance.

"You see, so much has happened, and it's been so long since…" She dragged a hand through her hair, telling him she'd been doing the same for probably the last half hour. "Damn it, I need…"

Without a word, he scooped her up in his arms, recognizing his own restlessness as a desire to hold her. It was time to stop denying them both.

She sighed and melted into him, but it wasn't until her arms encircled his neck that his own body settled, for once content.

Gently, he brought her back to the couch. Sinking in, they lay curled, her back snug against his chest, her head tucked safely under his chin. Slowly he rubbed, enjoying the texture, the smell. Needing to comfort, needing that comfort.

The rightness seeped in, catching him off guard.

Little by little, the layers of muscles relaxed. His, hers. Until she sighed again, then his arms tightened. "How long has it been, Gypsy, since anybody's held you?"

"Jon did, once. When we said goodbye. A big bear hug. It felt good. Other than that, no one since our weekend in your cabin."

"And Grace?"

"You know Grams, she loved me, but she wasn't one to…" She stopped and shook her head. "Cain, I didn't leave you because of the choice you made. I agreed with it."

"I know."

"We would've never been happy. Not really. Funny thing is, Jon saw it, too. He sat me down like a father would, to ask me if I was sure about being married to you."

"I could see him doing that." He sighed, not liking the raw feeling invading his chest at the mention of Jon's name.

Without thinking, he started rubbing the hollow between her shoulders, where he suspected the muscles refused to unknot.

"Mercer recruited me, you know. In fact, he recruited both Roman and me just as we were finishing our final year at the Naval Academy. Roman because of his diplomatic connections, and me—well, let's just say I proved I could handle myself even back then. That, along with the MacAlister name, caught the government's interest."

Cain breathed in her scent, no longer fighting the impulse, absorbing it easily. "When I started with Labyrinth, I began distancing myself from my family, friends. Partly because of the lifestyle and, of course, because of the risk. At first it was difficult, but over the years, with each mission, it became easier and easier until I couldn't break free, didn't want to. The scum of it eventually sticks to you like thick crude oil, to the point where you feel you'll never be clean."

"You can't change who you are, Cain."

"You did."

"No, I was no more than a lump of clay, molded into who I was told to be. Rather than take the risk I might be my mother, I became nobody really."

The carefulness of her statement, squeezed at his heart. He absorbed that too, as he did her scent, but this time, not so easily.

"You were always Prometheus. You probably came out of the womb with fists raised," she said.

He felt her smile against his arm and enjoyed the humor. Her humor.

"Jon recognized that in you, Cain."

"Maybe."

"Definitely." She leaned back and stared at him for a minute. Her face pale, like smooth milk glass, making the blue of her eyes softer—a rich sapphire velvet. Still, he noted the small lines of fatigue etched around her eyes and mouth. Remorse shadowed his conscious. He'd done that.

"That's why I let you believe I'd died, you know. It was the only way to protect you," she whispered.

Foolish, stupid even, but Cain still felt the slight

warming beneath his heart. In her position, he would have done the same.

"I didn't think you'd grieve too much, because I knew you didn't love me, not really, Cain. But your sense of duty to protect—engaged or not—would have made you stay."

"I understand." And it frightened him, that he really did understand. And more importantly, forgave. "You did what you felt was necessary."

"I was still clutching your mother's ring when the firefighters found me." She turned back, snuggled in deeper. "I kept it because for a long time it was my lifeline. But now…" She took a huge, shaky breath that trembled against his chest. "If you want it back…" The courage was there more than ever in that one simple offer.

And the love.

It was the latter that tugged on him—the deliberate, gentle tug of the inevitable. And God help him, in that moment he slid, slow and easy, into its warmth. "No. Keep it. It's yours." Needing more, though not sure why, his hand eased over her arm, grasped hers, palm to palm, fingers locked. *It has always been yours,* he mouthed the words silently against her hair.

She shifted her head until her cheek lay over his heart. He felt moisture dampen his shirt and recognized the tears for what they meant. The fact that she'd trusted him enough to let go humbled him, making his tumble that much more amazing, and that much more terrifying.

He'd taken on the Mafia, drug cartels, rogue agents and terrorists. Fearlessly, systematically. But for the first time, Cain tasted uncertainty.

After a while, the rhythmic breathing against his forearm told him she'd fallen asleep.

Gently, he cupped the back of her head, holding her to him. He placed a soft kiss on her brow, let his thumb caress the silkiness just under her ear.

The T-shirt's tag had flipped, sticking out of the neckline, Cain recognized the brand as his favorite. One that was no longer manufactured.

She'd taken his T-shirt from the cabin with her.

"You sure pick the damnedest time to go soft on me, Gypsy." Amused and frustrated, he closed his eyes—knowing he wouldn't find rest so easily. What the dregs of the world hadn't managed in over a dozen years, fate had handled in less than twenty-four hours.

A tiny gypsy had brought Prometheus to his knees.

A HIGH-PITCHED WHINE hit the air like a raid siren. Cain hit the deck, one arm protecting, one hand reaching for his pistol.

"A fax?" Celeste struggled off the couch, her eyes blinking away the sleep. "Jon is the only one with this number. Not even Olivia has it."

By the time they reached the second bedroom, a paper lay in the machine's slot.

"A photograph." Her fingers trembled, her face paled to white linen. But when she looked at Cain her eyes were ice-blue and steady. "Score one for the bad guys."

With a curse, Cain snagged the picture.

It showed the clear lines of a woman lying in the snow, her eyes open, the pupils flat and lifeless.

Cain scanned the picture until his eyes locked on the

lower right corner, knowing instantly why Celeste's hand had begun to shake.

According to the time stamp, the picture had been taken less than three hours prior.

"She's dead." Celeste leaned against the wall and looked up at the ceiling, trying to check her emotions. The soft tick, tick of a watch was the only sound echoing through the room.

Automatically she glanced at Cain's watch and froze. "Your watch is digital."

"Yes. What has that—"

"Shhh!" Celeste swung around, her eyes searching.

When Cain stepped closer, her hand held him back. "Bomb." They both started searching then, but it Celeste who found it.

"The fax machine."

"Get out of here, Gypsy," he growled.

"No!" She rounded on him, snapping fingers impatiently. "You still carry that penlight?"

When Cain didn't move, Celeste yelled, "Damn it, Cain. You may have handled my death by reinforcing your car against explosives, I handled it by learning how to disable them. Give me the light. Hurry!"

Cain reached into his pocket and pulled out his keys, then disconnected the penlight. He punched the red button, turning on the light. "Leave the black button alone."

"Why?"

"Because it triggers a laser. I sure would hate like hell for it to touch an explosive."

"Good call," she agreed with derision and directed the light to illuminate the underside of the fax machine.

The bottom had been removed from the machine to allow several small squares of a clay-like substance to be tucked up underneath the casing. Celeste shifted, feeling a thin sheen of sweat form on her brow. "Get out, Cain. He's got this thing loaded with C-4 explosives."

"Not on your life."

Hearing the hard edge on his statement, Celeste didn't waste any more breath, and instead pointed the light into the paper feeder. She saw it then, an analog wristwatch fastened to the back inside corner. The feeder triggered the watch to start its countdown. They had a minute at most. But worse, wires ran across and down each seam. "Damn it! He's rigged the whole thing so it can't be opened."

She jerked him away. "Let's go!"

They both hit the apartment door, scrambling. Half-way down the outside steps, they jumped the railing.

The store shattered, windows and frames exploded, showering them with splinters of glass. Instinctively, Celeste covered her face and sprinted blindly, held tight in Cain's grip. Before she could think, a second explosion—its blast hot and angry— shoved her into Cain and pelted them with wicked blows of wood and cement.

"YOU'RE LUCKY, Miss Pavenic. Just a bad sprain." The paramedic, a thirty-something-year-old blonde who'd look more comfortable holding a surfboard in his hands than a stretcher, finished bandaging Celeste's right ankle. "You should be as good as new if you take it easy for a few days and ice it every so often to keep the swelling down."

"Thank you." The throbbing had eased into a dull ache with the light compression of the wrap.

The paramedic stepped to the side and started putting his supplies away. "I understand your refusal to go to the hospital right now, but I would have it checked within the next few days."

"I'll be fine." Slowly, she slid off the back of the ambulance, testing her leg. "See?" Earlier, the paramedic had given her his jacket to stave off the biting wind. Now, she zipped it until the collar closed around her neck. She managed a tentative smile as she limped away from the ambulance, grimacing at the sharp pain only after she'd turned away.

Cain appeared at her side, and steadied her with his hand cupped at her elbow. "Going somewhere?"

"I've nowhere to go, or haven't you noticed?" Cain had foregone a coat, still wearing only his shirt and jeans to protect him from the cold. Other than a few facial cuts, he showed little evidence of their ordeal.

"What do you have on the woman?" she asked, knowing Cain had spent time on the phone while she'd been checked over.

"A Detroit prostitute by the name of Joyce Raines." Cain paused. "Age thirty-two. No relatives, no permanent address—other than her pimp's—and no worldly possessions except a cell phone—again, paid for by her pimp. Ian's hit a snag with the phone records."

"What snag?"

"There are no records," Cain spat. "Phone company doesn't understand how it happened, of course.

Roman's on it now. He's checking for back doors— it's only a matter of time before he finds something."

Celeste knew Roman's expertise lay in computer technology. "Could be our missing link. Whoever set me up used the cell phone to do it. I'm betting it's no coincidence. Whatever happened on that phone call might have cost Joyce Raines her life."

"Quamar's come up empty in Detroit. No witnesses, no leads. Other than her drug addiction, Raines led a sad, uneventful life." He handed her his PDA to read the details herself.

Quamar was also heading up to Shadow Point, something Cain had decided to keep to himself for now. It certainly wouldn't hurt to have someone else around to help keep an eye on Celeste. Cain couldn't ask for better back up than Quamar Bazan. Mercer had recently contracted Bazan for Labyrinth after the ex-Mossad agent had helped Cain save Roman's and Kate's lives the previous year.

"Joyce Raines." Sorrow shadowed Celeste's eyes, dimming the blue. She took another look at the PDA, but not before Cain saw the muscle flex in her jaw. Had he ever cared for people that much? "Just another statistic, isn't she?"

"Whatever she was, Gypsy, she didn't deserve to be murdered."

"Did you notice the list of items that are being held at the warehouse for the Cambridge auction?"

"Yes." Not for the first time, Cain noted the strength beneath her strained features, her pale skin.

"I think we should take a look."

"Not we. Me."

"You?" Celeste's temper flared, but Cain watched as she managed to control her exasperation, just barely. At this rate, Cain decided, it would take her years to master the technique. However, he found it intriguing that in spite of her experiences, she still wore her emotions out in the open for everyone to see.

"I'll decide if I'm going, Cain. Not you," she said. "Gabriel is upping the ante with that bomb. He wants to see just how much we can endure, if we're smart enough to survive his tactics or scared enough to run. I'm not going to let him win, not when we've come this far."

"I'm taking you to my place." His hand tightened, halting their progress, his eyes catching a black shadow by the porch.

"Cain, what quarters did they find on Joyce Raines?" Celeste stepped forward, then froze. Her whole body started to quake.

"Kentucky." Following her gaze, Cain understood. "My old Kentucky Home."

Chapter Ten

The bastard had left it just for her. Only a few feet away from the front stoop of the store. Close enough to the burning building so it wouldn't be missed. Far enough away so the fire wouldn't touch it. He'd even dropped a blood-red bow from her shop on the body as if it were a gift.

She took another shaky step forward, her anguish palpable. Still several feet away, she reached out to touch the mangled animal. Cain stopped her, clasping her trembling hand within his when what he really wanted was to gather her close and take away the torment he saw in her eyes.

"I should've realized Gabriel would target..." the rest of the sentence caught on a sob.

In the background, a police officer's camera flashed systematically, catching onlookers for future scrutiny. Just in case the bomber wanted to enjoy his show. Soon, Cain knew, they'd take pictures of the cat. Something he wanted to avoid her seeing.

There was little blood around the carcass, which

meant whoever had killed the animal had done so somewhere else. Maybe inside the store. Cain looked up at the blaze as the firefighters fought to control it. The fire had climbed as high as the treetops, the flames stroking the blackened sky. A small crowd of people had formed—some neighbors, most strangers—forcing the deputies to push them back to a safe distance.

"I'll take care of it," Cain responded, gentling his voice. Looking again at the heap of raw meat, he forced himself to remain objective. Only a slight tremor of his jaw gave away the fury that brewed under his calm surface.

The cat had been decapitated, the head left by its partially skinned, mutilated body. The guts had been thrown like discarded streamers over the steps and sidewalk. Amidst the gore near the tail lay five quarters— all North Carolina, all flashing brightly against the black fur.

Gabriel had wanted her to be able to recognize her friend, and leave no doubt about the torture he'd suffered.

Cain pulled her to his chest, and forced her face away from the gruesome sight. "I'm sorry." This time the comfort came naturally to him, like breathing. Trouble was, he wasn't sure he liked this new side of him. The hate had been easier to handle.

A sob escaped her, muffled by his clothes. Lightly, he soothed her, his fingers tracing long lines of comfort up and down her back. "It's over."

Another sob, this one a vicious jab just under his heart, a heart he'd thought long ago had stopped feeling anything.

Celeste drew a shaky breath. "I can smell him even

through the smoke, Cain." Fur soaked with blood had a distinct scent. Sour. Tinny. Heavy. The grief raked her from toes to chin, laying her wide open to its pain.

"I want him autopsied. Tonight." Slowly, she straightened, stiffening her spine to keep from crumbling into a ball. "If Gabriel left something behind, even the tip of an eyelash, I want it found." She sidestepped Cain, to get a closer look. To remember every detail. Bile rose in her throat. She tasted the acid before beating it back down.

"I'll talk to the deputy."

She glanced at the burning building, though she no longer cared about her lost possessions. No longer cared that the rose and talcum that was Grams was gone forever with the ashes and smoke.

"Miss Pavenic, I think I might have found something that belongs to you."

Both Celeste and Cain turned as Sheriff Lassiter approached them.

A worn Stetson, a sheepskin coat and his long, easy gait only accented the sheriff's small-town persona. Not an easy feat considering that until a few months before Lassiter had been a city boy.

In his arms, he held a bundled rescue blanket, but it wasn't until he'd almost reached them that Celeste heard the angry hissing.

Pan!

With a cry, she reached for the cat, hugged him tight. Her fingers smoothed the damp fur while she instinctively counted the heartbeats beneath.

The answering mew, although irritated, sounded

healthy. Celeste offered a prayer for the animal on the ground a few yards away that hadn't been so lucky.

"Thank you, Sheriff," Celeste swallowed the knot of tears, that clogged her throat. "I don't know what to say—"

"Part of the job," Lassiter replied, shrugging. "I found him under the Dumpster in the alley. Put up quite a fight when I went after him." Lassiter pushed back the brim on his Stetson, and smiled gently. "If I were you, I'd keep a close track on your pet from now on. He's probably down a life or two."

"Probably, but thank you anyway," Cain answered, shaking the sheriff's hand and then nodding toward the blaze. "Have you found out anything yet?"

"The firefighters say that the flames caught hold of the lamp fluid stored in your stock room. Only took seconds after that." Lassiter looked up at the two-story inferno and scratched the stubble on his cheek with his knuckles. "They haven't figured out what caused the explosion though. Could have been a gas leak. Could have been arson."

Cain slipped his arm behind Celeste's shoulders. When she tried to shift away, his hand curved her hip, stopping her.

"I hope you all don't mind if I ask a few questions." Lassiter tilted his head in the direction of the fire. "Like why someone would want to burn you out?" His lips flatlined. "Or leave a mutilated cat on your doorstep?"

"A burglary gone wrong?" Cain suggested. "We've heard there have been several break-ins lately.

"You did?"

"News travels in small communities. Especially bad news."

Slow to answer, Lassiter's gaze shifted from Celeste to Cain, intense and curious. "A mutilated cat adds a new twist, don't you think?"

"That's the problem. We don't know what to think, Sheriff." Celeste answered, cutting off Cain. The slight pinch on her hip told her he wasn't happy about it either. "The building exploded. Other than that—"

"Frankly, I'm amazed we got out alive. Once the explosion hit, we were running," Cain interrupted. "We gave our statements to your deputy."

"He told me." Lassiter paused long enough to rub the back of his neck. "You know, I've only been in town a little over two months, and I've seen more action here than during my last six months in Detroit. Whoever's behind these burglaries is leaving one hell—" He coughed, covering his slip. "Is leaving a mess."

"Any leads?" Celeste asked casually.

"None. Despite the mess, the places have been clean. No evidence. The trouble is that robberies rarely happen in Shadow Point, so people don't have security systems or surveillance. Most don't even lock their doors at night."

Celeste stiffened in defense of her neighbors. "Most have lived here all their lives and don't feel it's necessary."

"Yet, you did," the sheriff speculated. "Didn't you, Miss Pavenic?"

"Yes, but I haven't lived here my whole life, either."

"Funny though, them firefighters over there told me that someone would've had to be pretty savvy to breach your alarm system. Now, why would a thief target a store with a security system, when another with a dead bolt is just a block away? And why would he break in while you two were enjoying your dinner upstairs?"

"I'm not an expert, but maybe this particular one preferred a challenge."

"Maybe," he agreed, but his narrowed eyes said he didn't. "But why isn't your system set to notify my office when it's breached?"

"I felt safe enough that the extra precaution didn't seem necessary, Sheriff."

"Next time, you might want to consider it."

"Next time, she will," Cain responded easily, intentionally cutting off the sheriff's questions. "But for right now, I think we both need to regroup."

Lassiter paused, then nodded his agreement. "I'm sorry about your store, Miss Pavenic. But I promise you, I'll get to the bottom of this." He turned away, only to swing back again. "Do you folks have a place to stay?"

"We haven't decided—"

"She'll be staying with me," Cain said, then slid his hand into the soft curls at the base of her neck. "I've rented a place just south of town. Your deputy has the address."

Her arms tightened in surprise. Pan screeched and struggled to get free. When one claw found it mark, Celeste gasped.

Smoothly, Cain grabbed Pan and bundled him into the rescue blanket. "I'll keep an eye on her," Cain said, keeping his tone casual. "And the cat."

On cue, Pan popped his head out from between the blanket's folds, and Lassiter scratched him between his ears. If he thought it strange that Cain had his own place already, he kept it to himself. "That's good to hear."

"Once your investigation is finished, I'd be interested in knowing how the burglar got through the security system," Cain admitted easily.

"I can't make any promises." Lassiter glanced back at the roof engulfed in flames. "Looks like it's gone now, but I'll let you know what we find. Meanwhile, you folks be careful. I'm not convinced this is the end of things."

"We'll keep an eye out for anything out of the ordinary."

"I appreciate that." Lassiter nodded and turned away.

Celeste watched the sheriff amble towards his patrol car. "He didn't believe us," Celeste murmured, then rubbed noses with Pan, letting the warm velvet fur reaffirm that he was safe.

Cain's mouth twisted wryly. "Maybe we should have gone with the seagull story."

"First Grams, then Jonathon, now my store and Pan." She scratched Pan under his collar, eliciting a purr. "He's destroying everything personal to me. We need to warn Olivia Cambridge, Cain."

"Not yet, Gypsy. Not until we know for sure she's not behind all of this."

"We can't take the risk—"

"I'll make sure we boost her security a little bit, to cover our bases."

There was a loud crack, like thunder. Celeste jerked around just in time to see her apartment collapse into her store. Cain squeezed her into her side, reassuring her.

The gesture made her chest constrict.

"Cain, I want Gabriel," Celeste said, trying not to think of the blazing mass behind her. Instead, she concentrated on the coins and the stray cat that lay cold on the ground next to them. "I want back in my store first thing in the morning. If Gabriel left anything behind, I want to know."

"There's a lot of hours between now and the morning," Cain answered grimly. "I think we'd better put them to use."

"I agree," she said, this time taking comfort not from the *we* but from his arms. For the moment she was safe.

"Cain," she whispered, suddenly overwhelmed with the realization of what he'd done for her. Of how this evening could've ended.

"Hmm?"

A firefighter yelled. Another raced past. The savage looks on their faces told Celeste she'd lost everything.

Celeste gave herself a second or so to allow the words to unclog from her throat. She glanced up at the swirling snowflakes that danced in the wind above their heads. The more unfortunate ones were caught in the flames, their split-second sizzle echoing in the night air. "Thank you for saving my life."

"I haven't saved it yet, Gypsy."

She saw the cold determination cemented on Cain's features.

And loneliness took on a completely new meaning.

"No more, Celeste. You're done."

"Don't you ever get tired of bossing me around?"

"I wouldn't have to, if you stopped letting your emotions cloud your thinking. You're injured and that makes you a liability in a situation like this."

"You're not the team leader here, MacAlister." Exhaustion tugged at her, but she refused to give in. It had taken another half hour for the fireman to contain the fire. Once they had, Celeste and Cain had left. "I'm a trained operative," she added, ignoring the fact that her ankle still throbbed.

"A trained operative who spent all her time in satellite offices with very little field experience."

"The quarters were a message for me. You and I both know that the odds are he'll show up at the warehouse tonight." She thought of the North Carolina coins. "The airplane on the quarter? The airfield by the warehouse?" Her laugh ground to bitter dust in her throat. "Gabriel's not even trying to challenge us now."

Cain flicked off the headlights and slowed the car to a stop. The warehouse was a converted hanger located on the north edge of town, just past an old airstrip. The steel building sat a couple hundred yards back from the road with only some floodlights in the distance marking its position.

Still, she was annoyed when Cain switched off the ignition. "We could probably creep a little closer, don't you think?"

"What I need you to do can be done from here where you'll be safe." He glanced into the rearview mirror and saw Pan lying stretched on the seat licking his paw. "Besides, you have Pan back there to keep you company."

The cat stopped in midstroke, mewed, then continued his onslaught. Celeste ignored him, knowing the cat was biding his time. He didn't like being cooped up any more than she did. "How am I going to be any help here?"

"Look, Celeste, I need you to watch my back while I place the security cameras." Cain dropped the magazine of his gun, checked it, then slid it back into place. "Will you do that for me?"

"Fine." She spat out the word and permitted herself a withering stare. He was lying of course, but when he put it that way...

She folded her arms, furious at her vulnerability. The problem was, she was beginning to wonder if there was anything he couldn't do by himself.

Cain punched a few buttons nearby. "Let's see what we're dealing with."

A circular screen blipped. Within seconds of inputting information, a schematic of the warehouse superimposed itself over the original diagram. Cain used a small toggle to guide the tracking until it focused on the different areas. With a few taps on the keys, he zoomed in. "If we've jumped to the wrong conclusion and these burglaries are just a coincidence, then we've only assisted Lassiter in getting his guy. No harm, no foul."

"We're not wrong," she argued, still irked that he'd won.

Two white figures appeared on the monitor. "An RTI?" Remote Thermal Imaging Systems, used to track a person's body heat by satellite. She'd seen many like this one during her career with Labyrinth but always in surveillance vans, never in cars, let alone a Jaguar.

Celeste tapped the screen. "You've got two guarding the warehouse. I'm betting private hires looking for extra cash. Not any big threat for the great Prometheus." Celeste leaned over the screen, almost bumping heads with Cain.

"Don't tell me you're worried?" When his eyes found hers, the eerie green of the computer screen cast a sharp and very dangerous edge to his features. "Don't be." He held up a miniature camera, the size of a tack. "Planting the cameras is easy. In and out. Thirty minutes max."

"Why can't we just tap into the warehouse cameras?"

"Unreliable. I prefer my own."

"Easy or not, watch yourself." Her request drifted in a hushed whisper between them, thick with tension. "I've never lost a partner," she said.

"You've never had a partner." A sensuous light passed between them, and its implication sent unwelcome waves of excitement rolling through her. "Not like me anyway."

"Yes, well…" She cleared her throat, pretending not to be affected, before glancing again at the console. Both guards had remained stationary—one at the back of the building, the other in front. They looked like small white globs.

How dangerous could white globs be?

"Here." He handed her a small piece of flesh-colored, gum-like substance. "There's a small transmitter in the center."

"I've used them before. It amplifies my voice with vibrations so no one else can hear me but you. And vice versa." She took a moment to adjust to the foreign feeling of chewing gum in her ear. "If I think you need help, I'm coming in."

"Not unless I give you the okay. Agreed?" Cain took an identical one and placed it in his left ear.

She nodded toward the two guards on the screen. Let Cain think what he wanted. "Don't hurt them."

He quirked his eyebrow, an action she was becoming familiar with. "They're not the bad guys, Gypsy. I promise they won't even know I'm there. Just keep an eye out. The guards will patrol the grounds on and off. Even if Lassiter doesn't understand the coins' meaning, he's smart enough to beef up the patrol cars in the area. I'd like to avoid a run-in with a trigger-happy lawman."

"Watch out. He's rigging the bombs with analogs on purpose. And the access too. If he's planted a bomb in the warehouse, it'll be rigged to the door as well as a clock. You can almost bet on it."

He tipped her chin up. "Don't worry, I'll come back to you."

Maybe it was the words he used or the stress of the day. Either way, Celeste felt her emotional barricade give. Burying her face in his neck, she breathed a kiss against his skin.

Slowly, he pulled her to him until her face turned upward. "You pick the damnedest times to go soft on me, Gypsy." His mouth descended to hers. "We might just be by a bed next time." The last of his statement was smothered in a series of slow, shivery kisses.

"Don't be too sure," she said, when she finally came up for air. A small lock of hair curled against his fore-head. Not thinking, she brushed it back into place with trembling fingers. The gesture was familiar enough to make him pull back. Celeste masked her hurt, realizing it was okay for them to kiss, but he wouldn't allow anything remotely connected to caring. Heroes didn't become involved.

But she wasn't a hero.

"Be careful," she whispered, talking to an empty car. He'd already slipped into the darkness. It unnerved her how quietly he moved, because it reminded her of who he was—and more importantly—that he couldn't be anything else.

Pan's high-pitched meow broke into her thoughts. She glanced up to see him take a swipe at the windshield. "Don't start complaining."

Sitting on the dashboard, Pan looked at her, his black lids half-closed, his manner superior.

"I could let you go, but I'm not going to. So deal with it."

With a short, spiteful meow, Pan jumped to the back of Cain's seat. His fur spiked into little spears of hair, while his nails dug into the leather.

Celeste glanced at the small, puncture marks dotting the upholstery. Normally, she would've scolded him, but tonight she figured he was justified. "Feeling better?"

Far from it, she decided dryly, when the cat shifted slightly and flicked his tail.

"Gypsy." Cain's voice rumbled softly in her ear. "I'm in. Where are the guards?"

She studied the screen. "They haven't moved from their positions." Her eyes darted once again over the white figures. "I'm not reading you, Cain. Are you wearing an implant?"

"Yep. Otherwise, I'd be part of the crowd."

Celeste was familiar with the thermal diffuser chips, but never had needed to use one herself. Mostly because they were permanent, surgically inserted under the skin.

"Just let me know when their positions change. They should be making rounds soon. Until then, stay alert."

"You and I both know I'm too far away to do any good," she said while she scanned the darkness. "Wasn't that your plan?"

"No tantrums, Gypsy. I need you to keep up your end of the job. I don't like surprises."

She glanced at Pan. The cat was just putting the finishing touches on the upholstery. Grinning, she noted several additional holes in the leather. Childish? Maybe. Satisfying? Definitely. "My tantrums are the least of your worries." She scratched between the cat's ears in reward. "You just keep your end out of danger," she warned. "And I'll look out for the rest."

Having tired of his game, Pan settled into her lap and, from the satisfied way he licked his paw, seemed content.

"Gypsy, check camera one for me."

As she watched, the screen divided itself into a tic-tac-toe board. The top right block flickered then focused on one of the warehouse aisles.

"It's working," she acknowledged, her eyes searching for movement among the boxes and shelves.

"Copy that."

She studied the screen, then the outside. Cold fingers of fear stroked her spine and her muscles tightened against the sensation. She eased her gun from its holster and set it on the driver's-seat cushion. Cautious, she pressed farther back into her seat and waited.

IT TOOK one bullet from Gabriel's silencer to shatter the floodlight, blanketing the warehouse entrance in darkness. He paused next to the building, waiting patiently, listening. After readjusting his night goggles, he glanced down. The guard's lifeless body lay at his feet.

With very little effort, Gabriel shoved the dead man's back against the wall. The slap of his skull on the concrete echoed softly in the night air. Gabriel scooped up the flat-topped security hat and placed it back on the guard's head. The dark brim covered the small, symmetrical hole that tattooed the middle of his forehead—leaving the impression that the guard was asleep.

Swiftly, Gabriel tossed the man's gun, phone and other items into the brush before accessing the security panel, noting the age and uselessness of the system. Why is it, he thought, most people think things will never happen to them until they do? Thousands of dollars of merchandise in storage, protected only by some floodlights, a few cameras and an antiquated infrared system—the minimum equipment required by their insurance company.

He glanced again at the dead man. "They're making it too easy for me." He traced several wires, discovering someone had rerouted the main circuits. "Well, well."

After grabbing a small black canvas bag from the ground, he slid a six-inch blade from his arm sheath. With one swipe, he severed the wires. The interior lights blinked, then disappeared. The cameras went dead.

He slipped through the door and crept past some larger crates, tempted by the opportunity to torment his adversary. "Come out, come out wherever you are," he whispered, finding enjoyment in a game he was never included in as a child. "Whoever you are."

"GYPSY, give me the guards' positions."

Fifteen minutes. Celeste's heart pounded. Cain had planted half the cameras in less than fifteen minutes. Another half dozen cameras and he should be out of there.

"They haven't moved—"

The warehouse lights winked, then darkened in the distance.

Cain swore. "Gypsy, listen to me." She heard it, the worry. "I want you to stay—" A sharp buzz pierced her eardrum. She cried out, her hands tearing at her ear until the transmitter dropped into her lap. Someone had jammed the frequency. Her eyes locked on the screen, immediately taking in the two fading white blobs, and then a third, burning bright and moving unhurriedly toward Cain.

Gabriel. It had to be.

Desperately she tore apart the car, looking for a flashlight, night goggles, something to help her maneuver in the dark—only to come up empty-handed. The man had fifteen million gadgets but not one lousy flashlight.

Gun in hand, Celeste pushed open the car door and slid out, wincing when her injured ankle tried to take her weight.

Without a sound, Pan shot out through the open door.

"Pan!" she whispered harshly, but she was too late. The darkness swallowed him whole. "Stupid cat," she muttered, forcing herself not to worry. The wind flogged her, each icy lash cutting deep to the marrow of her bones. She glanced again into the night and clamped her jaw down on a frustrated scream.

In her mind, time accelerated, devouring precious seconds before she reached the first guard in front of the warehouse doors. She squatted, tested his pulse. None. She searched him for a flashlight, frustrated when she found nothing. Didn't anyone use one anymore?

She saw them then, the glint of metal in the moonlight. After scooping up the coins, she shoved them into her jeans pocket, not caring about anything except Cain's safety.

Hurriedly, she stepped over the body and slipped through the open door.

As shadows shifted—some merging, most separating into shapes—Celeste moved farther into the building, heading in the general direction of Cain's last location.

The size of two high-school gymnasiums, the warehouse was packed from front to back, bottom to top, with shelves, all overloaded with packaged goods. Most, she imagined, for the auction, others being held in storage for local businesses.

Pistol raised, the grip slick against her clammy hands, Celeste crept forward. So that is what caring for a man did to a woman? It makes her stupid with nerves. Carefully using the wooden crates and boxes as a guide, she worked her way through the maze of shelves.

A whoosh of air was her only warning.

A hand gripped her hair, jerking her head back. Fingers dug viciously into her scalp and cold steel bit her neck, cutting off her cry of alarm. "Drop the gun, Celeste." The knife blade pressed harder, its blade cutting her skin. "Gently."

Celeste felt the sting, the warm trickle of blood over her collarbone. Her gun slipped to the floor with a quiet thud.

"Or should I call you Lachesis?" The whisper taunted her, sending abrasive waves of fury over her.

"It's ironic really, don't you think? Lachesis being the Fate who determined the length of a mortal's life."

"If I had that kind of power..." she rasped, his vileness crowding her, suffocating her. "You can bet you would've never lived past your first breath."

Gabriel laughed, a grinding of vocal cords. "I must say, my night goggles certainly provide a nice advantage. I can see why Prometheus is smitten." He pressed closer, his chest to her back until she heard his black heart beating under her ear. A clammy sheet of moisture coated her skin, but she forced her mind to focus.

"Are you and Prometheus enjoying my game—"

Celeste relaxed, dropping her weight into Gabriel. When he caught her, the blade shifted away. She slammed her elbow into his ribs causing him to hiss and his hand to slide.

"Cain!" She ducked, aiming for Gabriel's groin. Within a fraction of a second he recovered, catching her punch, twisting her arm viciously until she cried out.

"Bitch!" He shoved her, chest first, to the floor and dug his knee into her spine. "Do that again and I'll break your back." The darkness disguised his features, but she'd remember the inhuman edge in his voice forever.

The warehouse emergency light flipped on, its red glare momentarily blinding her. Gabriel swore and threw off his goggles. Celeste hoped the shock of the light had blinded him, too.

"Looks like you got lucky. Tell your boyfriend to take better care of you. It isn't time for you to die. Not yet." A needle pricked the nape of her neck. He released her arm and stood. "But soon."

She tried to see him, tried to grab for the weapon lying only inches from her face, but a sick, malevolent numbness spread throughout her body. It was almost as if her circulation had stopped, leaving her muscles disengaged from her mind.

Seconds later—or maybe even minutes, she couldn't be sure—she found herself floating, cradled in massive arms. A fog, dark and thick, crept in, narrowing her peripheral vision. She tried to blink the mist away.

It was hard to make out more than the size of the man, but Celeste knew he was huge. An accomplice?

"No!" The word came out hoarse, so low she couldn't be sure he'd heard her. Talons of fatigue clawed at her, dragging her into a dark abyss. Struggling against obscurity, she tried again. "Cain!"

"Shhh. I am Quamar Bazan, Cain's associate. He is unharmed." The soft Mediterranean accent rumbled deep within his chest, a lullaby against her ear. "It is you we need to worry about."

Cain. Not harmed. With a sigh, she stopped fighting the crushing weight of fatigue, allowing her mind to drift with only one thought—if she didn't die now, Cain would certainly kill her later.

A SOFT, TWO-TONED WHISTLE floated to Cain. His muscles flexed but didn't relax. Softly, he whistled his response.

Cain heard nothing, not even the soft rub of shoes against the concrete before Quamar joined him, holding an unconscious Celeste to his chest.

"Is she okay?" The question came out in a short, savage snarl. Celeste's scream still echoed in his head, triggering the terror in his chest. Even as he'd hit the emergency lights, raced toward the sound—he'd known Gabriel had her, would hurt her. Known that he would be too late.

"She is fine. I checked her pupils and her pulse." Quamar shifted until her face tilted toward Cain. "It appears he drugged her. Fast-working, but harmless."

Fresh blood smeared her jaw. Cain moved the jacket collar a few inches, revealing the cut on her neck, a vivid red against her pale skin. Another reason to bring Gabriel down, he promised himself. Then he wiped some of the blood with his thumb, relieved when her pulse beat strong and steady beneath.

His eyes lingered, stroking her cheek, until he heard his friend clear his throat.

He jerked back, catching himself. "Get her out, Quamar," he ordered. "Take her to the cottage. And when you get there, see if these cameras can give us an image on the portable, although I'm sure they won't. I didn't have time to place any in this area. Check with Roman, too. He's monitoring from headquarters." Cain scanned the warehouse. "Our friend is long gone. I'm going to finish with the cameras, in case he decides to come back. I'll clear out before the law gets here or call them if they don't. It will give me time to…" He glanced at Celeste, his jaw tight, his eyes fixed. "…think."

Quamar's gaze flickered, sliding from Celeste to his friend. His broad lips widened with pleasure, his teeth gleamed, bright against his dark skin. "So you have become human after all, Prometheus."

"Don't worry," Cain ground out, not bothering to misunderstand. "I'll get over it."

Chapter Eleven

"Are you better, Miss Pavenic?"

Celeste angled her head, the closest she could come to a nod without having it implode. It had been a good five minutes since she'd come around, but she still didn't feel strong enough to move from her reclining position on an overstuffed blue-paisley couch.

"Do you have any aspirin?" She willed the parade of cannons to stop discharging inside her skull.

As he made his way to the bathroom, Celeste noted his tailored black slacks and black crew-neck sweater. Did everyone in this business, except her, have money?

Neither his clothes nor the confines of the cottage minimized the size of the man. He returned and dropped some tablets into her palm. She murmured her thanks and closed her eyes out of self-preservation. If she looked up at the man, her neck would stretch and her head would probably fall off before her gaze reached his chin.

"Is there anything else you need? Something to eat, perhaps?"

The thought of food touched off a wave of queasiness. Quickly, she swallowed the pills with the help of some warm tea. "No, thank you…" What did he say his name was? "Quamar." She frowned, struggling to find the whole name. "Quamar Bazan."

"You have a good memory, Miss Pavenic." The words were low, the accent heavy—and surprisingly soothing.

"Please," she murmured, wishing the aspirin would take effect. "It's just Celeste." The dread she'd felt earlier tried to reassert itself. Agitated, she rubbed her temples.

The man merely inclined his head as he poured more tea into her cup. "Then I insist you call me Quamar."

"All right, Quamar." She tried to smile. "How long did you say before Cain would arrive?"

"Soon. But there's no need to worry, he's in no danger."

Cautiously, she nodded her assent. "Cain. He's your friend?"

"Yes."

Celeste sighed, settling back against the couch. "And here I thought he didn't have friends," she quipped, only half-serious. She inhaled deeply, catching the light, spicy scent of the giant. Exotic, masculine. Pleasant.

"I never said he considered me a friend. Only that I considered him one."

She peered at him from beneath her lashes. "He must. He trusts you enough to bring you here. Trust doesn't come easily to him."

"Nothing comes easily to him except his job."

She acknowledged the truth of Quamar's statement. "You know him well." Deliberately, she took in the room, noting Cain's strong presence. Not his physical presence, although she caught a glimpse of his coat on the wall rack and newspapers on the table, but more of how the air was charged with him, like some sort of static electricity.

Startled, Celeste realized she'd come to rely on his energy. "Somewhere along the line, Cain's work became his life."

"Perhaps you should ask him why." He rose, the tea-kettle in hand, and walked to a light-paneled wall. He flipped off a switch leaving the room in a soft amber glow that emanated from the kitchen.

"Perhaps I'm afraid to hear the answer," she murmured.

Pine trimmed the stone-hewed fireplace, updated to burn gas, and accented the quaint cottage. Only a few feet from the couch, the muted hues of the fire mingled with the light, both complementing the cozy lines of the furnishings and the hand-cut ribs of the barrel-vaulted ceiling.

Like many cottages, there was a small but service-able kitchen, a booth-style table, and a bathroom on the opposite side by the bedroom. All clearly visible from her position on the couch.

Unlike most cottages, computers and surveil-lance equipment took up one corner. Scattered in piles lay gear and apparatus—some under counters, more stacked on top.

"You've come prepared." Quamar's graceful motions surprised her as he walked to the kitchen and reached into the cupboard for a small first aid kit.

"A precaution." Quamar shrugged, returning to

where she lay and sitting down on the coffee table beside the couch. "One of many."

Celeste watched him glance at the work station, monitoring the high-tech systems. Computers, radar tracking, satellite imaging, closed-circuit monitors—some she recognized, the use of others she didn't have a clue about.

"If you have to work—"

Quamar's gaze returned to hers. "I have set up the portable monitors but Cerberus is monitoring through a satellite feed, allowing Prometheus and myself a little more freedom to accomplish our mission."

"Cerberus?" It took Celeste a moment to remember. "Cerberus—that's Roman D'Amato. I remember." She nodded her head. "Cain has him watching the warehouse?" She asked, suspecting the answer before Quamar spoke.

"Yes." Slowly, he tilted her chin up exposing her neck. "The wound is paltry, but needs cleaning. Do I have your permission?"

"Yes." The throbbing ebbed, and Celeste managed to sit a little straighter. "The portable monitors are new. Are they another of Kate's inventions?"

The antiseptic wipe soothed the sting of the cut. The gentleness of Quamar's fingers soothed the tension everywhere else. "Doctor D'Amato is an extremely clever woman," he explained.

Something in the man's tone—some pride, a softness that seemed more than casual—caught Celeste's attention. "Does Cain know that you're in love with his sister?" She almost bit her tongue off when the question slipped out. She must be more exhausted than she thought because she usually wasn't so unfeeling. Or maybe Cain was rubbing off on her.

But Quamar surprised her with a grin before bandaging the wound. "You must be very good at your job."

"Lucky guess." Uncomfortable with the quizzical glint in his chocolate-brown eyes, Celeste focused on the smooth lines of the giant's bald head.

Something about the man conveyed trust, gentleness. She decided to be honest. "Look, I'm sorry. I'm not usually so callous. Your feelings for Kate D'Amato are none of my business. My only excuse is that it's been a long day."

"We all have our secrets." Then, with a chuckle, he sat back and studied her for a moment. "It is hard for one not to love Doctor D'Amato. Yet, because of this love, it is easier to accept that she has found happiness with a close friend."

"Is it?" she murmured. Celeste had known Cain would eventually love another. Even while she'd hoped as much, during the late hours of many nights, the despair haunted her.

"Prometheus hasn't realized that you still love him, has he?" After grabbing the first aid kit and wrappers, Quamar took them to the kitchen.

"No," she said, too startled by his question to offer any objection. "How did you guess?"

"Probably the same way you did." His laugh was marvelous—a thick, warm comforter to snuggle under on a dreary day. "It was not hard. Your eyes burn with a blue fire at the mention of his name. A fire that is not created from just anger or frustration."

"With me it's never been a question of love, Quamar. But acceptance." She did love Cain. "Too much has happened. Our pasts are too tangled. We've both changed." The admission came hard to her, and not without pain.

"Will you tell him?" Quamar asked, seemingly busy with his task, but Celeste wasn't fooled.

"That I love him?" She questioned, proud of herself for not letting the show pain through. "Probably. Will it matter?" She asked rhetorically. "Probably not."

His features gentled with concern. On most men his size, the expression would've appeared ridiculous, on Quamar it was genuine.

"We have an unpleasant history." Celeste sighed, her mind sweeping back through the years.

"And here you both are—how did you put it?" His smooth forehead creased as he struggled for the word. "Tangled." His mouth curved, victorious. "You are both still tangled."

"But in a different way," Celeste admitted. "An entirely different way."

Quamar nodded. "But when a person is tangled, there are only two options. Take the time to straighten the knots, or cut themselves loose, quick and clean.

"You do not have much time to decide." He nodded toward the kitchen window. "Cain has arrived. And…" he added as his eyebrow rose speculatively, "…if I am not mistaken, he appears extremely agitated." Quamar glanced over his shoulder. "You might want to consider cutting loose, Celeste."

When she frowned, Quamar laughed. "At least you would have a knife for protection."

CAIN PARKED and cut the engine of the Jag. In the distance, a dog barked, then after a second, came a few answering howls. For a moment, he listened, trying to find something to calm the storm within him. But in his mind's eye, Celeste lay unconscious in Quamar's arms, the red gash on her neck, her body limp.

The anger surged, fed by impatience and—damn her—fear. Celeste had managed to worm past his emotional barricade and left the need for reassurance throbbing in him. Reassurance that she was safe.

He glanced at the cottage, following the pointed peaks of its roofline to the clapboard siding and small-paned windows. The knowledge that she sat just beyond the glass did little to help.

On the surface, he appeared to be in complete control, even relaxed. But a caged tiger prowled within—held back with a fragile lock.

"Let's go, cat." Pan yowled as Cain pulled him from the passenger seat into his arms. "I don't want to hear any complaining." Cain shoved open the car door with his foot and stepped out into the cold night air. "You're going to owe me some leather, and I don't mind taking it out of your hide."

CELESTE DISMISSED Quamar's observation. Cain furious? Even if he was, he'd control it. He wouldn't allow himself to be so human. She stood though, wincing only a little over her stiff ankle, refusing to face Cain any other way. What she expected was indifference, even a scathing lecture on her incompetence—not that she would've tolerated it.

What she didn't expect was the rush of relief that hit her when Cain filled the doorway.

Quamar had told her Cain was safe, but until she saw it herself, she hadn't truly believed him. She caught the back of the couch for support and drank in the raw sexual vibrations, the rugged windblown features—the angry determination. She knew, ironically, that if he were to change, he wouldn't be the man she loved.

"I found your cat by the warehouse." Cain dropped Pan to the floor, showing disinterest when the cat scooted under the couch by Celeste. "You should do a better job of keeping track of him."

"I should—"

"Yes, you should." It ought to have been charming—just the thought he had rescued Pan, Celeste fumed. But then he'd had to open his mouth and ruin it.

He glanced at the monitors. "Anything?"

"No. Gabriel disabled the cameras," Quamar answered and shrugged on his down jacket. "I doubt he will return."

"Then we try again," Cain said. "Follow me." Before turning, he pinned Celeste with narrowed eyes. "You stay here."

Not waiting for an answer, the two men stepped outside. Celeste prickled with anger, forgetting her earlier worry almost instantly.

"I'm not your pet, Cain. And I'm tired of being told to stay." When she pushed the door open, both men turned in unison, like two vultures spying prey. Celeste took an involuntary step back, halted and stood her ground.

"I don't think you want to mess with me right now,

Gypsy." Each word was spoken low, each syllable drawn out.

She stiffened at the challenge. "Really?" She moved with a definite purpose, choosing to ignore her limp. The night air lashed out at her, piercing her shirt, leaving her skin a blanket of goose bumps. She crossed her arms, more in defiance of the man than the weather. "I'm not messing with you, I'm working with you," she responded tightly, annoyed when she couldn't stop the piercing shrillness of her comment. "You tend to forget that." God, he'd not only turned her into a loon, but a shrewish one to boot.

Quamar tilted his head back with a low, rumbling laugh. "I will head to the Cambridge mansion. It seems you have your hands full here. I will contact you if I discover anything."

"The mansion? To do what?" Celeste knew she'd be safer if Quamar stayed, but she refused to think of that now that he was leaving. She was not a puppet in this mission, to be pulled this way and that, whenever it appealed to Cain. If she hadn't warned him, he would've been knifed at the very least. And for once she'd like to see a little gratitude, damn it!

The slam of the car door brought her abruptly out of her thoughts.

"Quamar's going to scope the estate, see how secure it is." Cain watched as she rubbed her arms. "We can give Olivia a little more protection, without jeopardizing the integrity of our investigation."

"Why aren't we going with him?" she demanded, biting down on the urge to let her teeth chatter.

"I trust Quamar to take care of business." Cain's face tightened. "And as I pointed out before, you're injured."

She reached up and yanked the bandage off her neck, barely holding back a wince. "It's nothing more than a scratch."

"And your ankle?"

"I've run on worse," she countered, defiant, until a ripple of shivers ruined the effect.

Cain's eyes narrowed. "Get inside, Celeste. I don't need you to catch pneumonia on top of everything else."

"Don't worry about me."

"I wouldn't if you followed instructions."

"Instructions? Or orders?" With a huff, she limped past him, grateful to be back in the warmth of the cottage. "I told you, I can take care of myself."

"You're wrong." The chill in his words dropped the temperature inside to zero.

Cain locked the door, then lounged casually against the frame. "I told you to stay in the Jag." His comment was low, even lazy, but he didn't fool her. Not anymore. In the soft light of the room, she saw what she'd missed outside in the darkness.

Although his stance seemed relaxed, his eyes had narrowed into two slits of tempered steel. And she understood instinctively, if she moved, they'd slice her in half.

Quamar had been wrong. Cain wasn't angry, he was enraged. Containing a sudden surge of panic, she glanced at the doorway behind him and gauged her chances.

"Go ahead, try it," he taunted, crossing his ankles. "I'd like nothing better."

"You'd have come after me under the same circumstances." Silently calling herself a fool for not heeding Quamar's warning—for depending on Cain's innate self-control—Celeste stepped back, putting a little distance between her and the storm she saw raging in him. Somehow she knew, a simple grab and shake wasn't going to do him this time. "Admit it."

"I needed you monitoring the cameras," he countered evenly.

"Quamar said Roman was monitoring them, too."

He eased away from the door then, and took a step toward her, stalking her. "You didn't know that."

"I didn't know a lot, it seems." Her chin went up, as anger brought her a surge of courage. "You take risks all the time. I have the right to choose when and if I'll do the same."

"Wrong again."

She flung her head back, annoyed by the fact that she had to in order meet his gaze. "How was I supposed to know Quamar would show up? Why aren't you screaming at him?"

"Because…" He removed his jacket and tossed it onto the bench seat. "*He* followed my orders."

"You knew?" Of all the unbelievable… "How? I was with you every minute today, Cain."

"He and I made arrangements while you were dealing with the paramedic." Blood pounded in his veins, straining every muscle, every fiber of his being. Emotions he'd kept in check for an eternity rose to the surface.

When Celeste threaded her fingers through her hair in agitation, the movement caught his eye. Somewhere in that split second, he decided. This time, it would take more than simple eye contact to reassure him that she was unharmed.

"And you were going to tell me about these arrangements...when?"

"I wasn't going to tell you at all. Since he was wearing a non-thermal implant, you'd never have known the difference."

"I could've shot him!"

"*Not* if you had stayed in the car." Ever so slightly, he moved closer. Although they were still inches apart, she could feel the heat of his anger burning through her clothes, singeing her skin. "You made the wrong decision and risked your damned life because of it."

Celeste tried another step back, but her bottom hit the end of the kitchen counter. The dimensions of the room had shrunk in the space of seconds.

"Hold it!" She brought her hand up between them, regretting her action almost immediately when he caught her fingers.

"I did once," he murmured, then moved in, closing the distance, his eyes now smoky slits. "More than once. A thousand times, I've held back with you." He pinned her, imprinting his hard, long body against hers. "Not this time."

Her heart fluttered. If she didn't tread softly, she'd lose more than just this argument.

She'd lose herself.

"Look, I'm sorry you're upset with me for being in the warehouse, but nothing happened." She tried to maneuver away, but the edge of the counter bit into her back.

"Nothing happened?" A vein in his throat bulged, and

her eyes widened in fascination. How could she ever have thought this man lacked emotion?

"You're damn lucky." He gripped the counter on either side of her. "You could've been killed." Celeste watched his shoulders and biceps flex in an effort to maintain his temper. "Quamar was there to cover my ass, and instead he had to save yours. Dammit, we almost *had* Gabriel. I should strangle you just for that." His breath exploded in a hiss. "And for scaring the hell out of me."

"No!" Alarm skittered up her spine. Without thinking, she flung herself forward, shocking them both as her arms tightened around him. "Don't you see? I had to help you," she murmured and buried her face into his chest. "When the transmitter went out, and the guards were dead, what did you expect me to do?"

"Trust me." Cain's arms automatically jerked around her, gathering her closer. His anger dissolved with the pain in her admission. He stroked her hair, catching the familiar scent, using it to reassure himself she was safe. At least for now. "I expected you to trust me."

"He might've killed you," she whispered, her shame seeping through. She leaned back and Cain saw the sheen of tears. "I couldn't do anything else." Cain caught her sob against him and kissed the top of her head. She took a shaky breath. "I love you."

It should have stopped him. A wounded admission like that would've stopped him before. Hell, a thousand things would've stopped him before. Things like integrity, duty—simple decency. But not one of them was going to now. He'd known that when he'd locked the door. He'd known it the first time he'd kissed her. Hell, he'd known it the moment Mercer had uttered her name.

With a touch of his finger, Cain tipped her head back. The room's lights set the honey-gold of her hair on fire, drawing him like a moth to its flame. Gently, as if haste might destroy the moment, Cain ran one knuckle down the delicate curve of her throat, stopping briefly to feel the hitch of her breath.

"So beautiful." He dipped his head until his lips rested by the fragile shell of her ear. "You have only a few seconds to say no," he whispered, checking his control, before giving in to the temptation to taste.

A gentle finger touched his lips, cutting off his words. "Shhh." The word was carried on a sigh so soft it was almost a prayer. "I want you, Cain. Even if it's just for now."

The tightness in his chest—a tightness he hadn't realized existed—eased. He didn't like the fact that her decision was that important to him. Meant so much.

The change in the way Cain held her was subtle, but Celeste felt it. His arm flexed against her back, his hips shifted slightly away. She glanced up at the taut skin of his cheekbones, sharpening the angles of his face while the gray in his eyes swirled, twin hurricanes.

"Cain?" Her hands froze against his chest, paralyzed with fear. Not fear of the war waging within him. But fear of his withdrawal.

No! Her mind screamed. *Don't be the hero. Not now.*

Chapter Twelve

Celeste grabbed his head, tugging his hair, pulling him down. Her lips pressed against his, clumsy in their haste. The resistance was there, the way his mouth flattened against hers. But she would have none of it. She loved this man with every fiber of her being, and if all she had was this moment, so be it.

Boldly, she stroked the grim line of his lips with her tongue. She teased the corner of his mouth as he'd done to hers so many times before, only to pause long enough to nip sensually at his lower lip.

With a growl, he cupped her bottom and lifted her, holding her tight against him, leaving her feet to dangle inches above the floor. His lips opened over hers, capturing them with a tender fierceness that melted her bones into a waxy goo.

"Let me show you what seduction is," he murmured hoarsely. Without losing contact, he placed her on the counter, bringing their eyes almost level, and stepped between her legs until his arousal rubbed against the apex of her thighs.

Her surge of victory was brief, flitting away under the sudden onslaught of desire and nervousness. She'd freed the beast, but now what would she do with him?

As if he understood, he eased back, his gaze a soft caress. Gently, as if not to frighten her, he outlined her breast through the cotton of her shirt, each stroke of his finger setting off a burst of electric jolts through her. With a moan, she gripped the counter.

Cain felt her shudder, her hesitation. With deliberate movements, he skimmed the line of her spine, enjoying each shiver he set off. When he reached the base, his hands curved around the flare of her hips, lifted the T-shirt over her head and tossed it aside.

His gaze fastened on his ring hanging between her perfectly shaped breasts, blue ice against hot silk. A primal need burst through him.

With the tip of his finger, he traced the silver chain, fascinated as the goose bumps tripped over her skin. He let out a grunt of satisfaction that spanned a hundred years of his Scottish heritage.

"Cain." The raw plea came from deep within her, drawing his attention to the erratic rise and fall of her chest.

"No silk lingerie?"

With a jerk of her head, her eyes found his. "That was Diana."

Reverently, Cain rubbed the fabric of her bra between his finger and thumb. His hand hovered over the front, his knuckles deliberately brushing the swell of her breast, enjoying the contrast of the soft cotton and silky skin. "You make simple white cotton sexy, Gypsy."

Celeste's nipples tightened. A moan escaped her lips. "Wait!" The request came out more than a little frantically as she slipped off the counter. Cain deliberately allowed her body to slide against his until she touched the floor, causing another series of tremors. His or hers, he couldn't be sure. "My decision."

Riveted in place, Cain watched as she walked to the middle of the living room, dressed only in her bra and worn sweats. She pulled the drawstring loose, letting the waistband hang low on her hips, dipping slightly to reveal a hint of the shadow between the soft curves of her bottom. When she stood straight, her muscles flexed with a natural grace that made him taut with desire.

"My seduction," she whispered.

The serenity was there but still undermined by lines of tension as she slipped off her shoes and knelt on the sheepskin rug in front of the fire.

She closed her eyes against the heat of his gaze. Even from a few feet away, he caught how her fingers shook then fumbled slightly before releasing the catch. Slowly, she gripped the bra and pulled it away, freeing herself.

The silence was deafening, except for his own uneven breath. He stayed, mesmerized. Her breasts glowed like peach-tinted cream, the nipples dark, dusty-rose buds. She inhaled until her breath caught in her chest, exposing the delicate lines of her rib cage. The memory of her arching beneath him made his loins ache.

On a soft cry, her hands flew up in embarrassment, her eyes blinked open.

"Don't." His order was low, raspy—a man in pain. "I want to look."

His steady gaze, edged with passion, bore into her. With a shaky breath, he watched her drop her arms, leaving herself fully exposed.

The warm, burnished blush of the fire cast golden shadows, catching Celeste in a muted halo. The radiance made her skin appear delicate—almost translucent.

Graceful, strong.

He slipped the first button of his shirt free before he realized what he'd done.

Still, desire gnawed at him as his fingers hovered over the next button. He wanted to resist the pull, the urge to be with her. Hell, he might as well resist the urge to breathe.

Restlessly, Celeste ran her hand through the rug, caressing the supple surface. Cain's body grew heavy, aroused, spellbound by the sensual innocence that flowed from her. The second button slid undone.

"Cain?" Her request, though whispered, was simple.

With one tug, he freed his shirt from his jeans. A few seconds later, his shoes and socks lay on the floor.

He grasped the shirt fabric and yanked. The last three shirt buttons popped off. They hit the hardwood with a bounce and a rattle, causing her to freeze.

Before she could react, however, Cain was behind her, curling his body close to hers. When she relaxed, a surge of satisfaction rushed through him. He slid the bra off her shoulders and down her arms, letting his fingers trail over the silk of her skin. Only then did he reach for her, skimming the outside of her breasts before stroking the tips with his thumbs. He'd been the last to see her this way—burning with desire, aching with need. No other man had touched her since him. Like a double-edged sword, the thought brought satisfaction and with it, finely honed pain.

"You cast a spell over me, Gypsy. A curse, maybe."

Celeste's senses heightened with each word—forcing her to take a long, deep breath. A spell? Over Cain? A different form of excitement tripped down her spine.

She felt the brush of his shirttails against her sides, the warmth of his naked chest against her back. Hair, rough and sensual, tantalized the points of her shoulder blades, causing them to flex in greed, wanting more.

She slid her knees together to bring him closer, allowing his thighs to tighten against her in a ritualistic dance. No words were needed. Not here, not now.

He guided her hands to her belly, splaying them under his. Gently, he drew her back into him as he dipped then cradled her with his hips. As the hard length of him prodded her bottom, she shivered and gave in to the urge to rub.

She felt his hiss of pleasure on her neck, and layers of goose bumps spread. Then, deliberate fingers eased her sweats down, trailing in its path until they caught on the thin material of her panties. The deep, throaty entreaty triggered small tremors along her nerve endings, giving her a sense of power she'd never experienced before. Slowly, almost as though he was waiting for her to protest, he maneuvered her hand down the flat planes of her stomach, under her waistband, to the apex of her legs where her underwear was already moist with anticipation.

"White cotton?" He whispered, with a hopeful note underlying the question.

Her heart pounded, jumping from her chest into her throat, leaving her unable to manage more than a short, jerky nod. With gentle fingers, he guided her until they both massaged the ache building beneath the sable curls.

Flames of desire scorched her skin as they licked their way up and down her limbs. Automatically, she started to part her thighs, allowing more access.

"That's right, open for me, sweetheart." Her head fell back against his chest, as his fingers dipped and stroked. "I'll take care of you."

Take care of her?

"No!" She gasped, trying to harness some control even as she sagged farther into him. She tugged her hand free and turned into his arms. She fisted her hand to keep from stroking his fevered skin. "I want—"

"Me, too," he growled wickedly. "So let me." He took advantage of her hesitation to slip his hand under her sweats, his fingers traced the valley between her buttocks. Celeste's eyes closed, her head rolled to the side with a whimper. Wave after wave of longing swelled over her at the unexpected caress.

Cain captured her mouth, his tongue thrusting, plundering—savage in its intensity. For a moment she gave in to the rawness of the possession, the turbulence of his passion as it swirled around them.

He tried drawing her to him again. Immediately her other hand joined the first and pushed, breaking off the kiss.

"No," she panted, more than a little desperate. "I want more—"

His lips covered her nipple with a primitive possessiveness that left her weak. Long, liquid lines of desire traveled from her breast to her belly, only to settle like warm honey between her thighs. Heavens, she loved that feeling. She let her fingertips slide over his nipple hoping to create the same sensation for him and was rewarded when a groan rumbled deep within his throat.

"I want control," she said, surprised at the rawness of her voice. She realized that more than anything in her life, she wanted to seduce Cain, the way he'd seduced her at his cabin—making her mindless with passion, making her fall in love. "All this time, you told me I needed to trust myself. But you were wrong, Cain. I needed to discover myself." She took a deep breath. There was still a chance for her to grow whole again. Something she'd never had as Diana.

He drew in a long, ragged breath then lowered them both back—catching her against him as they settled onto the sheepskin rug.

"I'm an equal. Yours. Quamar's. The people here in Shadow Point." The admission came from the darkest pit in her being. "I'm someone who matters." *I'm someone worth loving.*

Cain tilted her chin up until their eyes met. He kissed her lightly, tenderly, before laying his head back onto the rug.

"Good." She blew the word out on a long breath. Before her courage caved, she bent forward until their bodies touched. Slowly, she slid upward, hearing the hitch, the hiss just before her lips touched his ear. "Let me know what you like," she murmured, then she nipped his ear.

"That's a good start." Cain's face remained rock-hard, his features giving nothing away. He stroked her neck, tracing its delicate curve with his thumb.

Her pulse leapt under his caress. "Don't," she said, jerking back. "It's my turn."

"Okay, sweetheart." He shrugged, but Celeste wasn't fooled. When he locked his hands behind his head, the veins popped, the muscles bulged. She smiled with wicked delight, more than up for the challenge he'd just presented her.

Pleasure purred through her at the thought of taking Cain to his breaking point. "I think…" She deliberated a moment as she sat up, wiggling just a little across his groin. "I want to kiss you."

She trailed a delicate finger over his stomach, satisfied when it clenched beneath her touch. "Here." She stopped at his waistband and unsnapped his jeans. She tugged on the loose end of his shirt. "Comfortable?"

When his gaze fastened on her bare breasts, her heart nearly stopped but her nipples tightened. "Gypsy—"

"My turn," she said a little bit shaky, before standing. She didn't risk a glance in his direction. Nonetheless, she felt his eyes burn her as she slowly slipped out of her pants and underwear. It had been easier years before. Cain had always taken control.

Her courage had come from the heat of the moment. But now…

For a second she just stood there, lingering—not to tease, but because her legs wouldn't move. When her gaze finally caught his, there was an untamed, almost ruthless, flare of passion in the gray depths. She was surprised she was able to stand under the blast of heat, but in a blink it was gone, replaced by a hooded, almost sleepy gaze. Which somehow, Celeste decided, was just as dangerous, if not more so. "Man, Cain, you're sexy."

Her tone was like raw silk whispering over his skin.

Hell, Cain groaned silently, she'd barely touched him. But the words...desire thrummed in his veins, thick and hot.

Once again she straddled his waist, this time with her back to him, giving him an unhindered view of her beautiful derrière. His fingers flexed with the urge to cup the round curves, stroke the sensitive skin again. With one slow scoot she moved down onto his stomach. He could feel the brush of her minklike curls against his navel, smell the scent of her arousal. Cain locked his fingers together in a fierce battle for control.

When she unzipped his pants, he arched his hips, more in reaction to the butterfly touch of her fingers than to help her along. With one gentle shove, she pushed down the pants and briefs to his thighs.

He heard her gasp as his erection broke free of its restrictions. When she hesitated, leaving his jeans still halfway down, he knew those same fingers were going to flutter over his arousal.

Her breath hitched, her body tightened.

"Gypsy," he warned, his voice raw, his body desperate for a few seconds of reprieve. If she touched him now, there was a good chance he would embarrass himself. "It would be easier for me, sweetheart, if my jeans were completely off."

She looked over her shoulder, her expression sultry

and determined. Somehow, Cain sensed, her nervousness had disappeared, drowning under a waterfall of self-confidence. That in itself made this sweet torture worth it.

A moment later, she tossed his clothes aside, leaving them both naked. She faced him then. "Ready?" she asked, desire smoking her words. She crept forward, brushing, sliding until she was astride his chest.

His body throbbed, his heart pounded. Still he didn't touch her, but the effort cost him, as small drops of sweat beaded at his temples.

Taking a lesson from Cain, Celeste traced a small pattern on his biceps before moving to the inside of his elbow. When his muscles flexed then bunched in response, she couldn't stop the female satisfaction that rolled through her.

Riding that wave, she leaned down and parted her lips a mere inch away from his mouth until their breath mingled, hot and moist.

He was tight and aroused beneath her. She'd never felt more powerful in her life, more sensual.

Or more fragile.

"Cain." She chewed his bottom lip just a bit. A growl rumbled deep within his chest and triggered soft vibrations against her thighs. Celeste moaned and sank against him. He smelled of sex now, hot and sinful. "Kiss me."

Cain's mouth covered hers, his tongue thrusting, his hands still locked behind him, his arms straining with the effort to keep his shoulders in the air. Celeste gripped his hair, holding on, devouring the spicy male taste that was him.

Sheer willpower saved her. She pushed against his

chest, not willing to give up her advantage. Still, when he eased back onto the rug, she slid her tongue over her lips for one last taste. Pleasing her, pleasing them both.

"My turn?"

The rawness in the question made her body hum. He'd asked—not told—and hadn't realized it. Secretly thrilled, she shook her head.

"No," she said, her eyes brilliant.

But Cain was on fire. Their kiss surged his body into an exquisitely painful arousal. He tried to concentrate on something else, to undermine the need. When her lips brushed his neck, all thoughts spontaneously combusted.

"I like the taste of you," she whispered against his collarbone before trailing smaller, more delicate kisses across his chest. "Spicy, dangerous." Her tongue swirled around his nipple, and desire clawed at him, causing him to arch slightly from the floor. Where in the hell had she learned that?

Cain felt, rather than saw, Celeste shift down onto his thighs, her hands trailing behind her hot, little mouth as she moved. When she stopped, he could hear her breath grow heavier as she studied his arousal.

"You're so beautiful," she whispered, reverently.

Cain ground his back teeth, willing his body to obey his mind. Willing his mind to ignore what his sweet Gypsy was about to do.

Neither worked.

Her lips brushed the very tip of his arousal.

"Gypsy," Cain moaned, just short of demanding—for her to stop or continue he wasn't sure. Didn't care.

She'd heard him, he knew, but had ignored the plea,

intent only on her exploration. She shifted her weight until she lay lengthwise on his legs, her hips automatically gyrating against him as she moved.

Cain closed his eyes against the desperation rising in him.

Her fingers, cool and slender, cupped him, her thumb stroking the soft skin underneath. He felt the ring's cool metal as it drifted over his heated skin. His body shook, grasping at the slippery edges of control, discipline—anything.

"They feel like velvet. Soft, thick velvet." Her breath hitched. Then her lips touched them.

Cain shot up with the force of a missile, his hands still locked in place. That was his mistake. Because just then he watched her mouth, still swollen from his kisses, close over the length of him—moist, warm, sweet.

A moan rose from the very depths of his being, only to explode from his lips in a burst of longing.

Celeste looked up, her throat constricting at the almost feral look in Cain's eyes. A whimper escaped her lips, low and harsh—helpless as her core contracted in painful need.

"Cain?"

His eyes burned, he gripped her hips. With one fluid motion he hoisted her in midair, waiting for her to look at him. When she did, she gasped at the primal heat, the fierce possession and reveled in it. Roaring her name, he impaled her. She cried out with pure animal pleasure.

He surged forward, touching the very tip of her womb, touching the very tip of her heart. Emotions overwhelmed her. His, hers, both. Fever-pitched, she raked her fingers along his stomach, demanding he appease her monstrous yearning. He pulled out then plunged back in. Flesh inside flesh. Tight, hard. With one final cry, her body clenched, shuddered then exploded, her climax consuming her.

Only then did Cain give into his need. With another deep, almost savage, thrust, he came, shouting her name once more—the passion eradicating all but one last coherent thought.

Mine.

Chapter Thirteen

Quamar Bazan cursed silently at the damp weather that stole the heat from his blood. He adjusted his dark knit cap, pulling its edges over his ears. During his life, he'd spent many evenings in the cold, for the Sahara without the sun was like a bitter woman—frigid and steadfast in its vengeance against man. But when that same man gazed upon stars that blanketed the desert sky, well…

One glance told him no stars would appear anytime soon over Shadow Point. Allah was allowing nature a darker path tonight. So be it, he thought. The time would come when he could once again return home to the desert and his people.

In the distance, the dull roar of the wind rushing through the trees caught his attention. It is the way, Quamar mused. Life sometimes hastens on its path, stirring up man and nature along its way.

He slipped over the eight-foot stone wall surrounding the Cambridge estate. Pulling a cigarette-size tracking stick from his backpack, he hit a button to extend the prongs and stuck it into the ground under some bushes. On the tip, a small satellite dish beeped its activation, ready to feed perimeter readings back to Cain and headquarters.

Quamar grunted as he grabbed another. Concealing the sticks along the property boundaries would make it unnecessary for him to breach Olivia Cambridge's mansion. Quamar preferred it that way. He had no desire to disturb an old woman from her sleep.

Slowly he made his way across the area, his pattern a simple, direct line, his senses alert for patrolling guards.

He smiled in the darkness, a secret smile, as he swept through the brush soundlessly, measuring the distance, watching the reading feed into the small computer in his palm. Even though Quamar acknowledged the necessary equipment, he found more pleasure in the simple nomadic life of his tribe.

Unlike Prometheus and Cerberus.

His friends, Quamar had learned over time, did nothing simply. The concept was foreign to their driving nature. Why should love come to them any differently?

The scent of tobacco drifted through the air and Quamar slipped into the shadows just before the heavy step of a boot cracked a nearby branch. Quamar shook his head in disgust as he watched the red glow of a cigarette bounce through the night air as a guard passed by. It seemed Prometheus was correct. Breaching the mansion would be child's play, especially to someone of Gabriel's caliber.

Deciding he'd given the guard enough time, Quamar stood, checked the grid and gauged the next perimeter point.

Mid step, the pain him hit like an ax, cleaving his skull from crown to chin. Quamar dropped to his knees. He absorbed the shock and tried to stand. Another swing of pain—this time leaving stars—jagged with razor-sharp points—bursting behind his eyes. Bile thickened his tongue, even as the ground rose to meet him, cold and hard like a slab of concrete.

Through it all, Quamar felt the wind, its soft edges hastening past.

Then he felt nothing.

THE MOON broke free of the clouds, holding off the soft hues of dawn. A thin streak of light trailed across the walls, giving Celeste her first real look at the bedroom. She was surprised to find that it was nearly wall-to-wall king-size bed—sturdy pine with yards of breathing space and lots of wood.

In what little floor remained open sat a large oak dresser, a matching nightstand—and beige. Beige comforter, beige curtains—she tipped her head over the side of the bed—beige carpet. All understated in their elegance, and all accented with rich, earthy-brown walls. Simple, masculine.

Celeste gazed at Cain, who sprawled across most of the bed, his arm trapping her waist. Sometime during the night, he'd pushed away the warmth of the covers, leaving the sleek lines of his body naked to the cool air that danced in the room.

He'd had called her Celeste. Not Gypsy, not Diana, but Celeste. In his sleep, he moved his arm. His hand cupped her breast. From top to toe, goose bumps ran amuck, and in their wake came a series of slow, sweet shivers. She bit her lip, suppressing the sigh that threatened to slip past.

Even while he dozed, she sensed the barely controlled power that lay coiled in long, lean muscles. The man was a contradiction in terms. Lethal yet safe, powerful yet gentle.

Her gaze skimmed over the scars that patterned his back. Celeste ached to know what had happened, but she'd have to ask. And something she'd seen before in Cain's eyes—dark, wicked shadows—had warned her not to. He would never risk sharing that much of himself with her.

Cautiously, she touched one of the hard lines. A knife wound that hadn't been there the last time she'd last slept with him. A disfigurement that came with a history—one that ran much deeper than the skin, one that ripped through the soul, leaving unfathomable ramifications.

A past that had created the man.

She adjusted the down comforter, tugging the trapped corner from under her waist and pulling it to her chin. Sometime during the night, Cain had carried her to bed. The heat from their lovemaking had dissipated, leaving her slightly vulnerable and chilled.

No undying declaration of love would follow their lovemaking, now or ever. Even though the realization hurt, she didn't blame Cain this time. She'd taken the chance, had known the consequences. And in her heart, she knew she'd do it again.

Just as she knew he wouldn't.

A fist pounded the front door, startling Celeste. In an

instant Cain was awake, his feet planted beside the bed, his gun leveled, his body naked. "Stay here."

He pulled on his jeans, only pausing long enough to zip them, swearing when the attack on the front door continued.

As Cain stepped from the bedroom, Celeste grabbed one of his sweaters lying by the bed—time permitting only accessibility, not modesty—and slipped it on, grateful when the hem fell just past her knees. Seconds later when she joined Cain, Sheriff Lassiter was standing on the porch, his face blotchy with irritation, his frown turning his eyebrows into one bushy line. White plumes of breath puffed from his mouth as he talked, reminding Celeste of a spotted dragon.

"I want some answers, MacAlister."

A very angry dragon.

"It's five-thirty in the morning, Sheriff," Celeste responded. "Couldn't this have waited a few more hours?"

"No, it can't." The blue eyes, now rimmed with black fury caught hers over Cain's shoulder. "The car your fiancé raced against yesterday was stolen."

"It makes sense," Celeste said, then glanced surreptitiously at Cain. "Kids probably joy-riding after boosting a car."

"I would agree, but this car had more than a dozen 9mm slugs embedded in it. You wouldn't know anything about that would you?"

"No, we don't," Cain said easily and leaned against the doorjamb, his body blocking any movement of the sheriff's to step inside. "Why don't you ask the truck driver who spotted us racing?"

Celeste's hand slid easily over the warm skin of Cain's back until she hit the cool metal tucked safely in the waistband of his jeans.

"I wasn't asking you, MacAlister." Judging from the early hour, the sheriff's shadow of whiskers and red-rimmed eyes, Celeste figured on that top of everything else, the sheriff wasn't happy about the extra work hours he'd probably put in. "Let the lady answer for herself, if you don't mind."

"I do mind. The lady has been through hell in the last ten hours." Cain's arm tightened on her waist, drawing her to his side. She leaned in and allowed him to support most of her weight.

"I don't know about any bullets, Sheriff," she stated.

"No one's made any threats to your person in the last twenty-four hours? No one, let's say, who might want to torch your store?"

"Even *if* someone had," Celeste replied carefully, "I'm sure you can appreciate that we don't want to accuse anyone without proof."

"Since it's my job to investigate arson, I believe that's my call, isn't it?"

"I think—"

"I'm sorry, Sheriff," Celeste inserted, when Cain took a step forward. Her hand stopped him in mid-stride. "I'd hate to see what the media would do if they got a hold of my name and Cain's connected with unsubstantiated charges of arson."

"Look. Don't talk to me about the media," Lassiter snapped. "The day hasn't even started and already mine is in the crapper. I'm not much in the mood for games.

Besides your fire…" He jerked his thumb in the general direction of town. "I finally nabbed the burglar who's been ripping off people. Except I find out that not only has he killed two security guards out at the old airstrip, but, as we speak, Olivia Cambridge is lying on a slab down at the morgue with a broken neck. Strangled with her own damned necklace."

Horror slithered through Celeste, coiling deep in the pit of her stomach. Cain's body tightened, ever so slightly. Celeste felt it only because she was still against his side. "Olivia Cambridge is dead?"

"Stone-cold." Lassiter shoved his hat back on his head. "And the media you're so worried about won't be interested in you. In fact, I'm sure that every reporter within a two-thousand-mile radius is racing here to get the scoop on the president's dead mother. Can't keep something like that a secret. The only consolation is that someone put a bullet in the guy before he escaped."

"Who?" The question came from Cain, short and flat.

"The guards. A partner. Who the hell knows? The guards were firing at shadows when my deputies got there. Olivia Cambridge was lying in her study, dead and our killer was lying out on the lawn, bleeding a river from a head wound—jewelry spilling from his pocket."

"What time?"

"A little over two hours ago." Lassiter's eyes slanted, suspicious. "Why?"

"She must've interrupted a robbery," Celeste guessed, realizing that the sheriff hadn't mentioned any coins. Either he was keeping it a secret or there hadn't been any.

Maybe Quamar—

"I've seen stranger," Lassiter responded, his gaze resting pointedly on Celeste. "Like the fact..." He switched his attention back to Cain. "...that only a few hours before, Miss Pavenic's building was torched. And let's not forget the mutilated cat left on her doorstep—and, by the way, preliminary forensics have found nothing on that."

"The timing could be nothing more than a coincidence," Cain answered, his tone and his expression both smooth as glass.

"I don't believe in coincidences. Not in my jurisdiction. Especially when a foreigner who looks like a reject from the World Wrestlers' Foundation, ends up shot on the president's mother's front lawn."

"A foreigner?" Celeste made her question seem nothing more than casual curiosity. But a deep-down dread twisted the muscles of her stomach.

"A male, approximately six-six, late thirties to early forties, bald. Nationality undetermined. No identification, of course. In his car or on his person. That would make my job too easy." He paused for a beat. "You two wouldn't know him by any chance? Or you've maybe seen him around town? Or in that stolen vehicle?"

"No." Cain's answer was short, clipped.

Quamar? Shot? It took all Celeste's willpower to squelch her reaction. "You said he didn't die..."

"Not yet. But he is in surgery. Airlifted to Saginaw. Lucky for him some of the best surgeons in the country work from that hospital. But if he survives the night, I'll be surprised."

There was nothing they could do for Quamar, not

right now—except pray. One glance at Cain's rock-hard features, told her he'd concluded the same.

"Damnedest thing I ever saw," Lassiter continued, pulling his ear. "Whoever this guy was, he came prepared. He was wearing a knit cap that seemed to deflect most of the force of the bullet." The lines in Lassiter's face deepened with uncertainty. "I don't know about you, MacAlister, but I've never seen a hat, other than a military helmet, that could stop lead. I've sent this one to the lab for a breakdown of the material. If that cap was made here in the United States, I'll find out where."

"How about the security tapes from the estate? Do you have them?" Cain asked, seemingly unconcerned.

Lassiter grunted in disgust. "Useless. Somehow, he managed to breach the outside security system, then jammed the cameras. Found a whole bunch of electronic gadgets on his person and in his car. But all we got on the film is static. By the time her personal guards noticed and reached Mrs. Cambridge, it was too late. Seems they were paying too much attention to the Red Wings game and not enough to the monitors. Complacent bastards."

"What's going to happen now?" Celeste asked, already working through the possibilities herself.

"You're kidding right?" He snorted. "The news is slowly leaking out in town which means the media won't be far behind. I imagine once the president gets the message from the governor, who I notified a while ago, he'll be flying in to see to his mother. They'll put a cap on the information going out. They've already shut down the airspace within a hundred square miles of

Shadow Point. Besides the Secret Service, I'm sure he'll be bringing the FBI, CIA, Merchant Marines—and anyone else he can think of to interfere with the investigation. And all I can do is wait for the circus to begin."

"I'm sorry we couldn't have been more help, Sheriff," Celeste offered, hoping to end their conversation.

"But you can, Miss Pavenic. Both of you can." His gaze encompassed them both. "Don't plan on leaving the area anytime soon. I've a feeling that somehow the fire last night ties in with the murder. And I might have more questions later."

"We're not going anywhere," Cain said easily.

"Good." Lassiter removed his hat. He hit it against his thigh, knocking off a thin film of snow before stepping off the porch. "And to think I left Detroit for this."

HER FURY had faded more quickly than she'd thought it would. Only grief mingled with the ache of self-contempt remained, thrumming quietly yet insistently. "I should've seen it coming." Celeste moved away from Cain and dropped into a blue gingham chair. She pictured Olivia, slender and frail, only a little bit taller then Celeste herself. At seventy-six, Olivia would never have had a chance in a fight with Gabriel. "Quamar—"

"Roman's checking into his status, Celeste." But Cain's voice was grim, his features arctic-cold. Whoever had shot Quamar would pay, Celeste was sure. "When he knows something, we'll know something."

After the sheriff left, Cain had called Roman. It seemed Quamar hadn't laid enough satellites to give them a good reading on what had happened to their friend.

"The sheriff didn't mention any quarters." Tired, she rubbed the tension from her temples and studied the ones she had retrieved from the guard at the warehouse. She handed them to Cain. "All New York with the Statue of Liberty on the back."

"Olivia?"

"Maybe," she acknowledged. "But why not leave more by her body?"

"Lassiter could've been withholding the fact they found more coins."

"Possibly, but I don't think so," Celeste said. "Not when he already has his suspect nailed. He'd mentioned the jewels, why not the coins? Especially when he would've put them together with the quarters found by the dead cat?" Celeste shoved her fingers through her hair. "Quamar must've come across Gabriel after Olivia Cambridge was murdered."

"Or Gabriel took him down right before." Cain pocketed the quarters. "*If* Gabriel is the burglar."

"It's logical. He sets a precedent with the other robberies, then kills Olivia under the same circumstances."

"To make her murder seem unplanned?" Cain frowned. "Are you saying she was the target?"

"She certainly could've been, but why play the game with us if he took care of Olivia himself?"

"He wouldn't have," Cain said. "Which means—"

"She wasn't the contracted hit." Celeste started pacing. "But the bait."

"Meaning her death was setting a trap for the real target."

"Don't you see? It makes sense. If you kill Olivia

Cambridge, whose attention are you going to get? Besides the media's, I mean."

"You're telling me Gabriel wants the president's attention?"

"He wants more than that, he wants the president here." Celeste stopped pacing, pausing long enough to sort through the facts. "Olivia's murder certainly exonerates the president as a suspect. No advantage will come for his career through the death of his mother. That makes him the victim." Her tone hardened, determined. "Gabriel wants the president. I don't know the hows and the whys or even the when. But the where will be here. An unanticipated trip to Michigan makes the president vulnerable." Her eyes caught his, absorbing strength from their tough, steady gaze. "You have to make the president listen. Tell him to stay away."

"That's simple." His sarcasm wasn't lost on Celeste. "After all, his mother's murdered with a Labyrinth operative found half dead on her front lawn. And to top it off, the woman who conspired to kill his son lives in the same town. A goddamn nuclear bomb wouldn't keep him away."

"You have to try."

"I need hard evidence, Celeste."

"You won't have it." Her chin hitched only slightly when she continued. "Most people thought President Cambridge wouldn't run for a second term after his son's death—that he'd roll over and die from grief. Instead, he got angry. Turned some of it toward me, but more importantly, he turned the rest of the anger against terrorists and other organized crime. The man's not going to back down. You know that, I know that and Gabriel knows that. If I'm right, Gabriel's counting on it."

"I see where you're going with this, Celeste, but you're speculating all of this—"

"The most logical reason to kill Olivia Cambridge is to bring her son to Shadow Point. With his father buried here, the president isn't going to allow his mother to be buried anywhere else. It's a guaranteed point of contact. One pre-determined by Gabriel." She stood, suddenly restless. Or maybe she'd just felt like a sitting duck in the cottage.

"And if you're wrong?" He'd asked the question calmly, but even so, Celeste felt a piercing chill.

"It wouldn't be the first time." She sighed. "But right now, this is all I have, and we're running out of time." Lord, she wished he'd do something. Berate her because she wasn't finding a definitive answer, wasn't doing her job. Scream at her.

Take her in his arms and lie to her that everything would be all right.

Anything as long as he did it with some kind of emotion.

"You need to stop him, Cain. The possibility that I'm right is too high for you to ignore me. Tell him that somehow I was involved with his mother's death." She rubbed the goose bumps from her arms, wishing it was just as simple to rub away the past. "That I'm on the loose, that his life is in danger."

"I'll decide what's right for the mission."

He didn't touch her. Didn't kiss her. Rejection stiff-ened her back, tensed her muscles. She wouldn't beg. Not for his forgiveness, not for his love.

Cain knew what she wanted, saw the appeal shadowing her face. He rolled his shoulders, resisting the urge to answer her silent plea, sure that if he did, she might be able to convince him to use her.

He'd done it so easily in the past, but now…

"I'm taking a shower." He tipped her chin up, ran a finger underneath finding comfort in the smooth, softer skin that hid there. He couldn't remember any other time he'd felt so beaten up. "Eat something. There's toast. Once I'm out of the shower, we'll go to the Cambridge mansion for answers." He kissed her forehead. He gave himself that, knowing it had to be enough for the moment. "We'll figure this out, Celeste."

He'd used *we* again. At least there was that, she mused as she slipped back into the bedroom. Not love, not even lust anymore. She had no doubt that only duty remained for him—that and the need to protect her.

She heard him start the tap running, and then the door to the bathroom closed. The quiet decisiveness of the sound triggered one simple question.

Just how long would that feeling last?

THE WATER was hot, abrasive. Deliberately so, to keep him focused.

Celeste was starting to trust him. The revelation brought neither anger nor shock—just acceptance. And the knowledge left him vulnerable.

The ring of his phone broke into his thoughts. With a curse he cut off the water, swung back the curtain and reached for his cell where he'd left it on the sink.

But he was too late. Celeste had a cup of coffee in her hand and was already holding the phone to her ear.

"Jon!" Her face went linen-white, her hand trembled. "No, I'm fine. Yes, he's been…I'm glad you're…" Cain stepped toward her when her voice died. "Here's Cain."

"Celeste!" Cain swore when she turned her back to him and walked away, her hand in the air, telling him to back off.

"Damn it, MacAlister. What's going on?" The hollow echo of the retort told Cain he was on a speaker.

Cain watched Celeste walk into the bedroom. With jerky movements, she started pulling on her sweats, his white T-shirt.

"From what we could tell, you had suffered an abdominal wound—" Cain told Mercer.

"Not about my injuries, damn it." Mercer cut him off. "If you're still angry about Celeste being alive, get over it. I want a status report."

"I'm sure Roman's told you—"

"I did." Roman's voice boomed from the background. "He wants your version."

"And Quamar?"

"Still in surgery, Cain." Roman answered again, the concern in his voice raw. Roman and Quamar's friendship was rock-solid, dating back to when an Arab rebel unit had targeted Quamar's tribe. Roman had helped save Quamar's people and earned the giant's loyalty. "I'll let you know as soon as I know something."

"Tell me what the hell is happening, Cain," Mercer rasped.

It took Cain less than two minutes to bring Mercer up to date.

"And Celeste—why in the hell did she sound shocked? You didn't tell her I was alive, did you?"

"No," Cain's answer came after a moment, but the anger was there. Live wires snapping in the air.

"You'd better deal with it." Mercer paused. "Damn it, it feels like my belly's on fire." The words came out on a grunt of pain.

"Have you talked to the president?"

"Damn fool," Mercer answered, his irritation back. "I tried to convince Cambridge to delay his trip to Shadow Point, but some damned idiot named Lassiter promised to release Olivia's body to the embalmer. The autopsy was simple and to the point. She died from a crushed windpipe. The broken neck came after. They're waiting for the toxicology report but expect it to come back negative."

"Cain," Roman inserted. "Cambridge's people have already made arrangements for the funeral to take place later this afternoon. Couldn't get him to reconsider the location either—something about the family plot being sacred."

Mercer coughed. Swore. Then coughed again. "I didn't agree, of course. But there's no talking sense to him this time. Especially since his advisors are pushing the schedule. Figure the sooner the better. So far, they've been able to apply some pressure and stopped the press dead in their tracks, but they can only hold them back for so long."

"If they deal with the situation immediately, there'll be less damage control later," Roman added.

"Air Force One is due in Saginaw soon, Cain." Mercer continued. "All other details are being kept under wraps for security purposes. Even the FBI won't know when he hits town until he does."

"No other way to persuade him?" Cain asked.

"Would you listen to anyone if it had been Christel?" Roman inserted quietly.

Cain ignored him. "Jon, Celeste believes Gabriel will make an assassination attempt. I agree."

"We all agree, damn it," Mercer bit out. "Did Celeste fill you in on everything?"

Mercer's question seemed innocent, but Cain wasn't fooled. Jon was searching for some type of reaction.

"Yes."

"Good."

"But we can't use her as a reliable source," Cain responded, although he'd already planned to provide an extremely detailed report. He wanted the case well-documented with Celeste's history and current involvement. This time he'd make sure she'd be protected from any future recriminations. "Not yet, anyway."

"I agree." Mercer's sigh was long, weary. "The president wouldn't listen to her even with evidence to back her up. This is personal."

"Obviously, the man is not himself," Roman commented.

"Not himself indeed," Cain acknowledged, then after a moment added, "Not surprising, considering someone is systematically murdering his family."

"At least he's not bringing Mora or the girl, Anna. No sense in putting the First Lady and their daughter in jeopardy too. The only one accompanying him is Vice President Bowden." Mercer replied.

"Risky." Cain didn't like it. Having two heads of state in the same place at the same time was just asking for trouble. Too much of a temptation for fanatics.

"Damned stupid," Mercer bit out. "And after Robert got over the initial shock that I was alive, I told him that. But president and vice president have been friends for years, and Bowden felt they needed to show a unified front. Terrorist threats or not. He spouted some Southern rhetoric about dignity and courage." Mercer's voice hardened. "I didn't buy it. Personally, he knows it's a good publicity move if the reporters do get wind of the situation. The man's as slippery as those damned water moccasins he was raised around."

"Jon," Cain said. "Is Cambridge planning to tell anyone that you survived the assassination attempt?"

"No, not until I officially take command again." He grunted. "Roman's in charge until further notice."

"Did Cambridge at least beef up the security, Jon?"

"Yes, but over Bowden's protest. Besides the president's permanent attachments, they're bringing up the Detroit branch of Secret Service." Mercer snorted in disgust. "The vice president didn't want any changes that would alert the public to the murder."

Both Cain and Roman knew there was no love lost between the vice president and the director of Labyrinth. Although he had no proof, Jon had always believed that Bowden maintained his own agenda—one that didn't necessarily take into consideration the best interest of the American people.

"The problem is, Bowden has a valid argument," Mercer admitted. "Damned Secret Service tends to trip over themselves during these unplanned stops. If they can't get their security measures in place a month in advance, they might as well send out an invitation to every crackpot in the country."

"We added our own little mix," Roman interjected casually, but Cain wasn't fooled. "Ian and Lara are on their way," Roman explained. "They're posing as Secret Service agents. One on Cambridge, one on Bowden. But even then I don't know if it will be enough."

"Lara? *She* knows you're alive?" Cain swore. "Who authorized the change in assignment?"

"I did." Mercer interjected just as harshly. "You shouldn't have told her I was dead, Cain. She could have been informed. No reason not to trust her."

"It wasn't a matter of trust," Cain argued. He knew that Roman, as Labyrinth's acting director, had the final say in this decision. "It was a matter of her temper. She's emotionally involved—wants to avenge her father." Cain's jaw tightened. "You felt you owed her this?"

"No. I felt *you* did." Mercer's voice sharpened into finely honed steel, showing the hardened structure of the man beneath, the man who had survived years of jungle warfare. "And she isn't the only one who's on a crusade." He paused, letting his barb hit home. "Or am I wrong?"

"Let's just hope you're not dead wrong," Cain responded tightly.

"Cain," Roman cut through the tension. "Kate sent you a special present with Ian. She's says you're to use it or she'll come there personally, pregnant or not, and kick your ass."

A warning edged Roman's statement and Cain understood it. Kate wouldn't be the only one doing him physical harm if he caused Roman's wife undue stress while she was pregnant.

"What's Ian bringing?"

"Some of Kate's smoke screens. The ones that filter high winds and stay put." Roman's smirk came over the line loud and clear. "And if I know your sister, probably a whole arsenal of other gadgets. Plastic explosives, some acid rope."

"You two need to be on your guard," Mercer interrupted. "Whoever wiped the records clean on that prostitute's phone had high connections. Even Cerberus here," the older man said, his voice roughening with exhaustion, "couldn't find them. I'll expect you to keep me apprised of the situation."

"Cain," Roman's voice came over the phone. "Before we let you go, have you found out anything else on this Sheriff Lassiter? I came across a glitch in his file, as though someone had been screening the data just prior to his move to Michigan."

"Other than his being suspicious about our involvement in Celeste's fire, nothing out of the ordinary."

Cain tightened automatically, finding Celeste sitting on the bed, her delicate features serene. More Diana than he'd seen in the last twenty-four hours. Quietly, she listened, her long, soothing fingers stroking Pan, who lay curled in her lap.

"I don't like it. I started digging deeper into the files,

running a check on everyone who'd be at the funeral. Someone changed information on Lassiter's file. I missed it on the first check, because of the security path. The method is similar enough to the hooker's cell phone records to make me suspicious."

"It's enough to question him. Get on the phone and have Lassiter detained at his office. We're on our way," Cain replied. "If what you say is right, there's a good chance he could be Gabriel."

"I want that bastard out of commission before Air Force One touches Saginaw's tarmac," Mercer ordered.

"I'll take care of it."

"One more thing," Mercer said, his voice grim. "I've put Celeste through hell, all in the name of patriotism. She doesn't owe me anything, especially loyalty. I don't take something like that lightly. Anything happens to her, I'll hold you responsible. Got me?"

Cain's eyes narrowed as he studied Celeste. "If anything happens, Jon, there won't be enough of me left to hold responsible."

If he hadn't turned away, Cain would have caught her wince.

Chapter Fourteen

The Sheriff's Department was small, simple in its furnishings. Metal chairs, metal desks. Tan linoleum floor. One window to each wall, some of their blinds at half-mast, most closed.

Nothing to distract from business, except for an occasional plant. Most of these were artificial, Celeste realized when she studied the bent palm tree in the back corner.

Certainly, there were no pictures of family in evidence. Not because the people who worked here didn't have family, Celeste deduced, but simply because there was no room. Every available space held stacks of papers or hanging bulletin boards.

One lone desk near the door survived the clutter, only because it held a tall, tarnished coffee urn, with enough dents to make her wonder about its efficiency. The heavy scent of burnt coffee grounds hung in the air.

"Can I help you folks?"

Celeste took in the blue suit, matching necktie and white shirt. The guy had Agent stamped all over him.

Secret Service and FBI people crowded the office,

some on computers, most on phones. It was hard not to conclude that they'd found a base of operation.

"I need to talk to Lassiter, where have you got him?" Obviously, Cain had pegged this guy as a no-nonsense, by-the-book agent.

"And you are?" The man was in his mid-forties with muddy brown hair cropped short enough to necessitate the use of a barber every week, but not enough to hide the dusting of gray. Tall and lanky, she thought, Jimmy Stewart with a Brooklyn accent. And, by the look from the shrewd green eyes, the man in charge.

"MacAlister." Cain flashed his identification.

"Sam Garrett. Detroit Secret Service." The muscles relaxed, just enough to appear comfortable, but the eyes remained sharp. "I've been waiting for you, MacAlister. Seems you have some friends in pretty high places." He turned his piercing gaze on Celeste. "And you are?"

"Celeste Pavenic," she said with care. It had been a gamble for her to come, but she'd insisted. Her face had never been made public, never reached past the White House. These might be Detroit agents, but within an hour, Washington Secret Service will be all over Shadow Point. By that time, she hoped, it wouldn't matter.

"I'm Mr. MacAlister's associate." Celeste held out her hand, something neither man had done. "I wish we could've met under less urgent circumstances, Agent Garrett."

He grasped her hand firmly, shook once and let go. "Well, to tell you the truth, I don't quite know why we are meeting, ma'am. I was just told when MacAlister here showed up, I was to give him access to Lassiter. But I find myself…curious—"

"Roe, get the hell out of here. Find that son of a bitch, MacAlister. I want answers. Now!" Lassiter's voice cracked like thunder through the office.

"That would be your friend," Garrett informed them, poker-faced.

A college kid came out from the back room. Sandy-haired, with a basset hound's brown eyes, his face flamed in red. "Agent Garrett, the sheriff is pretty pissed—"

"Roe, this is Mr. MacAlister." He nodded toward the young man. "Deputy Rowan Cash." Without waiting, he waved his hand toward Celeste. "I believe he and Miss Pavenic would like a short conversation with the sheriff."

"Not her. Just me."

Cain caught the stiffening of Celeste's body and grabbed her arm. He nodded toward a scratched-up door with Lassiter's name plate glued to it. "Is it empty?"

"Yes," Garrett answered, his brows raised.

Cain glanced at Celeste. "Stay in there and wait for me."

"I'll do no such thing."

"You're not watching this interrogation, Celeste."

"Try and stop me."

"Agent Garrett," Cain addressed the other man, but his eyes stayed locked on Celeste's. "Miss Pavenic is a civilian with no identification. She is under my protection, most likely from the man you know as Sheriff Lassiter. We believe he might be an assassin whose intention is to kill both her and the president." His eyes flickered over Celeste at her gasp.

"I'm making a formal request that you keep her under

security in Lassiter's office, with a guard posted at the door until I get out of the interrogation. Is that clear?"

"Crystal." Garrett nodded toward Roe. "Deputy Cash, stand guard over Miss Pavenic until Mr. MacAlister tells you otherwise."

"Yes, sir."

When Celeste turned toward the office, twin blue lasers sliced through him, but it was the desolation behind them that caught his gut. He'd pay for this later, but at least for Celeste, there would be a later.

Celeste slammed the door shut behind her with a tightly controlled shove. Garrett let out a slow whistle between his teeth. "Hell, MacAlister, I just met you, but the parting shot that lady just sent you—well, any other man would be a shriveled pile of garbage on the floor."

"I've handled worse."

The lift of Garrett's eyebrow told Cain he doubted it. "If that's the case…" Lassiter bellowed out another stream of curses. "…your man in there should be a piece of cake."

When Cain stepped into the interrogation room, he expected Lassiter to lash out at him. What he got was a long, dismissive look.

"What the hell do you think you're doing, arresting me?" Lassiter demanded to know, leaning back in a metal chair, his wrists resting on the matching table in front of him.

"Shut up, Lassiter." Cain's little inner voice was working overtime. "Tell me why anyone would be messing with your government files."

"How the hell should I know?" Lassiter glared at

him. "Maybe someone doesn't want me looking at things too closely. Maybe someone wants me out of commission." Lassiter snorted. "Maybe someone wants you chasing your tail."

Cain swore, because the comment hit too close to home. "It takes more than just one goddamn phone call to put you in jail, Lassiter. Your files have been changed. At a level too high for me to believe you're not—"

Cain blinked, running through the facts in his head. Without a word, he turned on his heel and headed for Celeste. When Deputy Cash saw him coming, he quickly stepped out of the way.

"What the hell is going on, MacAlister?"

"I don't know." Cain shot his answer to Garrett from across the room. "But I'm going to find out." He shoved the office door open, knowing before he did that his little voice had been right.

Celeste had disappeared.

Chapter Fifteen

Cain roared when he saw the open window. But it wasn't until he saw the sapphire ring sitting on the desk that he felt the swift slice of fear.

He snagged the ring, its metal still warm from her skin and swung around.

That's when he saw it. On the wall—a newspaper photograph of Jim Lassiter receiving an award. A little leaner, a lot more hair, the sheriff stood proudly erect next to chunky brunette Cain guessed to be his wife.

He glanced at the date. Seven years before. "Damn it!"

Cain grabbed Cash by the shirt and shoved him against the wall. "How long?"

"I don't know." Roe's Adam's apple bobbed—to the point where Cain almost shoved it down the boy's throat. "I didn't hear a thing."

"Damn it." Garrett's hand gripped Cain's. "Let the kid go, Cain. It's not his fault."

Cain swore and let his hand fall away, ignoring the deep ragged breaths from Cash. "Go release your sheriff," he ordered the deputy before turning to

Garrett. "Issue an all points bulletin on Celeste Pavenic. I want her picked up now."

"DAMN HIM!" Celeste veered off the main street into the alley, needing the air, the space to think—not caring the wrath she'd face for climbing out the office window. The wind slapped at her, streamers of ice pricking against her cheeks. Cain had no damn right telling her to stay this time.

Cain had made his point brilliantly. With Lassiter in jail, her role in this mission had ended. Jon was alive. And between him and Cain, they'd take care of the president. That was all that mattered, Celeste reasoned, trying to convince herself.

Not the fact Cain had withheld the truth even after they'd made love.

In bed they'd played at being equal. In careers, he wanted her to sit while he took care of things. Kept her safe, a token partner in a locked room.

No, she corrected. A nonperson in a gilded cage.

Diana.

The truce hadn't lasted long between her and Cain. But the fact was, it had lasted much longer than she'd expected. It had taken the phone—its ring signaling the next round.

On the ride into town, there'd been no words left—only stony silence. In the past twenty-four hours, she had tried logic, persuasion—and when neither worked—temper.

She gritted her teeth, acknowledging her temper hadn't quite lifted. Stubborn idiot, she thought and kicked a small stone, vaguely registering its clank against a Dumpster.

If Lassiter hadn't called Cain a stupid son—

Celeste froze, remembering the tone with which Lassiter cussed at Cain. She replayed Gabriel's curses right along with it.

It wasn't the same.

Celeste turned on her heel, the fear slipping through the temper, its edges teetering on real terror. "It's not Lassiter, damn it," she said aloud.

A hand grabbed her arm, a second later cold steel touched the back of her neck. "You figured it out too late, Miss Pavenic."

"TIME TO WAKE UP, Goldilocks." The words slid into the mucky haze. The timbre coaxed, even soothed, but when she tried to focus, it floated from her, leaving only confusion.

And the cold.

The chill slithered in and gnawed her limbs with sharp, icy teeth. From beyond the haze, she heard a low moan and realized the pitiful noise came from the back of her throat.

She tugged at her arms wanting to cross them for warmth, but her wrists were too heavy to lift.

"Wake up." Stars exploded behind her eyes. The impact threw her head to the side, jarring her neck. Pain shot through her jaw, up to her temple and burst through the top of her head. She cried out, but the sound was feeble, hollow. Blood seeped across her tongue—its sharp, copper bite mingled with the rancid taste of adhesive, gagging her. With effort, she swallowed the foulness back and forced her eyes opened.

"It's about time you came to," the voice quipped, its low, caressing tone contradicting the stars that continued to rake the inside of her skull.

Celeste blinked, until her vision cleared enough to focus on a curved iron railing. Deliberately she forced her gaze up, following the spiral of wrought-iron steps.

The lighthouse.

She struggled to rise, fighting off the last of the drug-induced fog. Cold metal bit into her wrists, throwing her off balance onto her side.

"Don't bother. You're handcuffed."

Celeste jerked her eyes toward the source, only to hear coarse laughter come from behind her. Celeste remembered that same laughter in the alley, then a sharp prick of a needle in her neck.

"Remembering?" He patted her shoulder, pleased.

She gauged from the shadow lengths that it had been a few hours since he'd kidnapped her. Gabriel wasn't stupid. He'd stripped her down to her T-shirt and sweats, left her barefoot, then positioned her strategically so that no one could see her if they peered in through the lower window.

"You're no lightweight, though. I'll give you that. It took almost the same amount to *kill* the prostitute. But she was already flying high on heroin." He leaned close to her ear. "Enough about her. Let's talk about…me." His laugh sent her skin crawling. "I suspect you'd like me to formally introduce myself."

The man who stepped in front of her looked more like a lawyer than a cold-blooded killer. He was no taller than six feet and the sun streaks in his shaggy blond hair under his knit cap were too strategically placed to be real.

With the black goose-down parka, he could have been mistaken for a yuppie jogger....

"How's your ankle feeling?"

Nausea slipped through her, thick and oily. She'd seen him before.

The paramedic at the fire.

"I see you're surprised." His lips were wide, but not overly thick, with only a hint of cruelty beneath his smile. "Maybe even a little disappointed?"

Celeste curled her fingers in her palms, trying to contain her rage.

"I wouldn't be so hard on yourself. After all, I've been at my profession much longer than you've been at yours." He crouched, putting his face mere inches from hers. No heavy beard line, no defining bone structure. An ordinary stranger who passed by on the street.

"It's amazing what roles a person can assume when he has access to the appropriate credentials. A definite flaw in our society now that we've become so advanced in our technology."

He stood, then stepped onto a nearby crate, jumping a little to test its strength before returning to Celeste's side. "You, of all people, would understand that, Miss Taylor."

He pointed to a thick eyehook impaled into the circular stairs above her head. "I'll have to position you soon, but first I wanted to thank you for making my job easier this time around."

Celeste tested the handcuffs.

"I suggest you use your intelligence." He reached over and caught her chin, his nails cutting into her jaw.

"It's been quite a game, hasn't it, Celeste?" With a knowing look, he released her, then threw a second crate on top of the first. The second he didn't test. "But it's not quite over yet."

A tear escaped down her cheek.

"Crying won't help." With his thumb, he smeared the drop, allowing his nail to scrape her cheek. The brown irises of his eyes remained empty, lifeless as stagnant water. "I've watched many cry. Men, women, children. In the end, they still died. Some sooner." His shoulder lifted indifferently.

The sting from the scratch fed her contempt, showing him the tear wasn't from fear but rage.

Gabriel's face tightened. "Defiance won't help you, either." Slowly, he slipped the thick noose around her neck. The rope lay heavy against her collarbone, then squeezed her windpipe as he pulled.

"And it certainly won't stop your death." He dragged her like a dog on a leash across the granite to where a large wooden lever protruded from the floor a few feet away. The rope's coarse fiber dug into her skin and her airway spasmed, but Celeste forced herself to remain passive, understanding that if she didn't move, she wouldn't strangle.

"See that switch? Here's where the final moments of the game come into play." He lifted her until she stood on the box, then tied the rope end through the eyehook. "I believe it's called Sudden Death." He wobbled the crates, causing Celeste to catch her balance. "As you can see your position's a bit precarious, so listen up."

Gabriel eased the knot—just. Air rushed in, burning her windpipe.

"I've given you enough rope so that if you jump and kick just right, you might hit the lever and stop the weight. Of course, you'll snap your neck—therein lies your choice."

"And if you miss?" He strolled over to the light-house's clockwork weight. "Don't worry, because underneath is an explosive—nitroglycerin—to make things a little more interesting. I love interesting, don't you?" He tugged on the chains. "Once the weight hits... well, you get the picture."

A violent shiver wracked her body—from cold or fear, she couldn't be sure. Celeste shifted, trying to keep her blood flowing into her arms.

"Oh, if you're hoping Prometheus will save you..." Gabriel started toward the door. "...so am I." He opened the door. "In fact I'm planning on it. You see, I've rigged the door to set off a remote detonator."

"Of course, to help you, he must succeed in killing President Cambridge for me. Otherwise, I won't tell him where to find you."

Cain? Kill the president? She shook her head. Never.

Seeing the gesture, Gabriel smiled. "Oh yes, he will." His eyes grew hooded, almost languid. "You thought you understood me? Understood the type of person I am?" He leaned against the wall, his arms folded. Lights and shadows harshened his features, showing them chiseled by years of butchery. "I played you from the word go.

"If *I* killed the president, I'd have to disappear permanently. Having someone else take the credit allows me to fade into the background for a while, then resurface at my leisure. This time there'll be no signature with the kill. No political statement to link me in any way."

Celeste understood. Gabriel had deliberately tied himself to a certain trademark all these years so that at the right moment, all he had to do was drop the trademark—go against type. No one would suspect.

"Nothing personal against you or Cain." He gave a thin, dangerous smile. "To make the ruse believable, I needed the best—Prometheus."

Celeste clenched her jaw, her body aching from the immobility. Her ankle throbbed from taking her weight.

"I read his government file. Found his vulnerable spot. You."

Celeste stiffened. That meant someone else had accessed Mercer's records and passed the information on to Gabriel.

"Once I realized you'd done me a favor by not dying the first time, Jonathon Mercer became my trigger and you became my bait. I'll bet you didn't know you were in Cain's file, too." Gabriel's tone was like ice. Celeste felt its chill slide into her and freeze her blood.

"After all, who could be more pathetic? A woman who was once Prometheus's lover and whom the president blames for the murder of his son?" He chuckled, the cold disappearing instantly. "Yep, a plan just can't come together any better than that."

His words were meant to wound, but they didn't. She was no longer the woman he described. No longer pathetic and weak. And she wasn't going to just roll over and die while Cain's life hung in the balance.

"It takes the weight almost three hours to lower completely. So you've got some time." He glanced at the noose around her neck, then pushed the lever. The gears clicked rhythmically in the air. "I disengaged the lamp, so no one outside will notice anything different. I don't want anyone disturbing you. Don't disappoint me, Celeste."

THE MESSAGE was blunt. The paper taped to his windshield. "Meet me on the ridge alone—or the Pavenic woman's dead. You have one hour."

The snow and sand should've crunched under his footsteps, Cain made sure it didn't. What little sun there was had disappeared. The fog thickened leisurely, encouraged by the lint-gray clouds that hung low over the horizon. In the past, the lighthouse lamp would've been activated, its solitary signal flashing in quick, short series—casting a warning out over the water.

Cain saw the silhouette of a man by the edge of the ridge, one foot resting on a small boulder, his back to Cain.

That in itself was meant as an insult.

Cain didn't care.

"Did you know that every lighthouse is set on a different flash sequence?" The voice floated across the distance. "To help the ships passing to chart their course." He shrugged when Cain made no comment. "Too bad ours isn't operational. Looks like it's going to be a bad day for the ships." The man glanced over his shoulder. He was just a few inches shorter than Cain, dressed in a dark parka with the hood up. What wasn't covered by the hood lay hidden beneath a ski mask. "But a good day for a burial. Don't you think?"

"What I think is irrelevant."

"True." Gabriel studied the lake, his hands in his pocket, his head to one side. "Did you know the word *Prometheus* means foresight?"

Cain didn't blink, didn't move—didn't buy into the act. "I'm not here to share tidbits of trivia."

"No, just making an observation." The man chuckled before stepping toward Cain. Without a word, Cain raised his arms and Gabriel patted him down, looking for weapons, recorders. They both knew he could take his time. He was in charge, the one in control.

But Cain was patient. This game he knew, understood.

Gabriel stood, satisfied Cain was clean. "I'm assigning you a labor."

The Greek term for task was not lost on Cain. "You want me to ensure your assassination of the president succeeds or you'll kill Celeste." The wind blustered about, gusting with fury, spraying mists of snow from the frozen edge of the water. Still, the force of nature dimmed in comparison to the rage building in Cain.

"Actually, *you're* going to kill the president. Today at the burial."

Cain mentally shrugged. It could've been either scenario. "And if I don't, Celeste dies."

"And in considerable pain."

Cain's stomach clenched at the comment, but outwardly he showed no emotion.

"You don't seem surprised."

"Very little surprises me." Cain forced his jaw to

relax into a deadly smile. "Besides, you left the coins on the guards at the warehouse. Lady Liberty is Celeste. Or am I mistaken?"

"The Cambridge burial takes place in an hour." Gabriel laughed at Cain's raised eyebrow. "My client keeps me well informed. But it leaves you very little time to make arrangements to attend—if you haven't already."

"And if I can't?"

"You could always ask your brother, Ian, to sneak you in."

Cain allowed astonishment to flicker in his expression and Gabriel grunted with satisfaction. "Don't underestimate me, MacAlister." The brown eyes narrowed dangerously. "I haven't gotten where I am by being sloppy. Your choice is simple. You can kill the president and save the woman. Or they can both die. I'd just have to disappear for a long time. Not something I want to do, but sometimes sacrifices are necessary."

"If they die, you wouldn't be able to go deep enough to hide from me."

"I wouldn't hide from you. I wouldn't have to." Gabriel's tone went arctic. "Didn't I mention you'll be dead, too?" The man shrugged, changing moods like a chameleon. "Frankly, I could've killed you several times—the lighthouse, the car chase—even on Main Street in broad daylight."

"Instead, you kept me interested."

"And we both know that protecting the Pavenic woman did the job. The woman has made you careless."

"Or maybe I figured the woman would lead me to

you and allowed myself to be played." He lifted a negligent shoulder. "After all, here we are."

"Certainly a possibility. But somehow I don't think you wanted it to go this far." Gabriel shifted, his eyes narrowing on Cain's bland expression. "You understand, there's no reason for all of you to die. I'm not getting paid for that."

"And the bottom line is money."

"Of course." Gabriel's tone remained matter of fact. "I leave all that patriotic crap to you heroes." He glanced up as small flakes of snow began to fall. "Now, I have Celeste in a somewhat perilous position. If you don't kill Cambridge by the time he leaves the cemetery, you won't have time to save her."

"I'm listening."

"It's simple. Even for you. Get near enough to kill him. The *how* is your choice."

"And his Secret Service kills me."

"You're a smart man, Prometheus. Utilize your brother. I don't care. My client wants Robert Cambridge dead. Whether you survive or not doesn't interest me."

"Tell me who hired you."

"I would except my next client might frown on the fact I can't keep secrets."

"You could rely on repeat business." Cain shrugged off the urge to attack, to see Gabriel's blood flow. "After all, you murdered Bobby Cambridge for this client, too. Didn't you?"

"Did your girlfriend tell you that?"

"She didn't have to. It's logical."

He tipped his head back and studied Cain's face for a moment. "Maybe."

Cain didn't flinch. There were different ways to play chicken. "Very few men could've pulled off that kidnapping and gotten away with it."

"Now you're flattering me."

"Someone wants Cambridge out of the White House. A mental breakdown over the death of his only son should have—would have—brought most men to their knees. Unfortunately for you, Cambridge has a will of iron. The kind forged from years of war and service to his country."

"Yeah, he's a regular patriot."

"And that leaves you only one choice now, doesn't it?"

"Not me, my friend. If it had been up to me, I would've killed the whole family. Been more profitable."

"Why the statement? Why not kill him in an accident?"

Gabriel's lips thinned into a feral smile. "My clients have bigger egos than we do, Prometheus. They prefer flash to subtlety. I please them when it suits me. Or when the money's right. This time it happens to be both."

"When I kill Cambridge, I'm just supposed to take your word that you'll free Celeste."

"You have no choice." Gabriel paused, feigning astonishment. "You aren't suggesting that I might not be trustworthy, are you?"

"It takes a high-ranking contact in the government to forge law-enforcement files and erase phone records."

"You have no idea," Gabriel said coolly. "I've left evidence with my client. It shows you and your friend

Bazan's involvement in not only Olivia Cambridge's murder, but the Pavenic woman's also."

"Evidence I'm sure they'll find once I kill Cambridge."

"Only a small challenge for someone of your caliber," Gabriel reminded him. "By the way, I have front-row seats at the burial today. So I'd better see lots of blood when he dies. That way there'll be no doubt." With one last glance at the lake, he walked past Cain. "Remember, the woman has only a few hours left. Don't disappoint me."

After a couple of steps, he stopped and faced Cain one more time. "And Prometheus. When you report back to Mercer, speak kindly of me, would you?"

THE SHADOWS grew long and jagged, creeping forward like the Grim Reaper. Raw fury fed what little strength Celeste had left. She yanked on her restraints wincing when the steel gnashed her wrists, shredding more of her skin and leaving the warm, steady trickle of blood on her palms.

She shifted her feet, giving her bad ankle a respite and automatically easing the throbbing in her calf.

The gearbox stood beside the lever, while inside, the steady click of the mechanism ticked its countdown.

FOREST HILL CEMETERY was larger than most would expect for such a diminutive population. Fortunately for security purposes, it was also located past the western edge of town and fairly isolated by a small forest. Hence the name, Cain thought wryly. Rows and rows of cement markers, various shapes and sizes—all pristine, most bare of flowers—stood serenely behind a five-foot wrought-iron fence that stretched around a four-block radius.

Just as Gabriel had predicted, Cain had no problem securing an invitation to the burial service. The problem would be getting close enough to the president to kill him.

His eyes skimmed the perimeter from behind mirrored sunglasses. In one glance, he spotted a dozen state troopers patrolling the area, others in sniper positions. The Cambridge family plots were located in a lavishly manicured garden beside the cemetery's mausoleum. Lassiter, along with several deputies and a few agents, were positioned on the roof of the weathered building, their rifles sighted on the spectacle below.

A damp, murky mist shrouded the hills, providing a dramatic backdrop to the discreetly plain but large drum-shaped mausoleum that stood alone amidst the cluster of pines and dormant maple trees. Constructed of cut limestone and covered with leafless brown vines, the mausoleum appeared nearly black with age. Two curved staircases, ornamented with various religious symbols, flanked opposite sides of the double oak doors, winding from the ground to the roof's flat surface.

President Cambridge stood near the newly dug, oversize grave. Oversize, Cain decided, to match the opulence of the more weathered gravesite of the president's father.

Snow dusted the ground and the scent of fresh, wet dirt hung heavily in the air in spite of the wind that gusted and swirled around them, stirring coat tails and flapping pant legs in its wake.

President Cambridge was tall, distinguished in a charcoal-gray overcoat with a subdued shirt and tie. His brown hair, peppered with gray, was cut tastefully close and neat, and although time had thickened his chest and waist, at fifty-five, the man was the epitome of elite.

Beside him, stood the slighter, shorter vice president, his thinning straw-blond hair standing at attention in the wind. Bowden's long, sleek Armani overcoat showed a peculiar contrast to the president's less showy attire.

There was a third man at the head of the gravesite. A slightly hunched, plump man in his late fifties. He was dressed in black, a white strip of cloth displayed in the open collar of his coat.

"We are gathered here in prayer for our dearly departed sister," the reverend intoned, raising a gloved hand toward the suspended mahogany casket while the other held a small, red Bible. "Olivia Ruth Cambridge."

Of the Secret Service, nine men and one woman surrounded Cambridge and Bowden. For a moment, Cain studied his brother, the largest of the dozen Secret Service agents. Ian, opposite in looks from his siblings, had cobalt eyes, hidden at the moment by sunglasses, and their father's chestnut hair, cropped militarily short.

In the distance a wail sounded, like a baby crying. Cain bit back a curse, knowing better. Pan was cheerfully shredding the rest of Cain's leather upholstery and letting everyone within earshot know it. At first, Cain had thought about leaving the damned cat behind, but for some reason he couldn't. Pan was the only thing Celeste would have left after this mess. Now, as the howling continued, he wished he'd thought harder about it.

Cain caught Lara Mercer in his peripheral vision. Slight in build and of average height, she wore the standard black Secret Service suit and still managed to stand out from the other agents. Her hair flashed red even with the lack of sunlight. She'd bound it tightly to the crown of her head, accenting her refined features and bringing out the riot of freckles on the otherwise flawless skin. But Cain knew that under those freckles existed a competent operative…when she curbed her emotions. Efficient and reliable.

Removing his sunglasses, he gave the signal, hoping that for this mission, she'd stay that way.

Lara and Ian slipped their hands into their pockets. Cain braced himself when they pulled out their fists and watched as the coffin was slowly lowered into its hole. With a flick of his wrist, Cain hit the detonator on his watch.

Simultaneously, three sheriffs' cars, no more than two hundred feet away, exploded. The ground shook, the Secret Service yelled as they dove for Cambridge and Bowden.

Chapter Sixteen

Chaos hit Forest Hill Cemetery.

Smoke bombs exploded, mingling with the rich, dark clouds from the burning cars. Ian and Lara had taken care of the protection detail—leaving them in thick, green curtains of smoke that defied the wind currents.

Behind Cain, shots sounded, the distinctive pop of specialized bullets from Ian's and Lara's guns. The veterans screamed for coverage while the less experienced scrambled in confusion and others coughed—their eyes red and tearing, their throats clogged with the smoke. Several agents lay at Cambridge's feet, unmoving, leaving their chief vulnerable.

Grimly, Cain launched himself, tackling the president and propelling them both into the grave.

Cain heard the grunt of pain, the whoosh of air as Cambridge landed back-first onto the casket. The instant Cain's knife filled his hand, he buried it, hilt deep into the president's chest. He heard the squeal, the sharp intake of breath. A sound that had almost become a litany for death during Cain's years with Labyrinth. Only this time, a good man exuded the noise. He pushed that thought away and pictured Celeste in his mind. Without hesitation, he yanked the blade clean, then forced himself to bury it again.

Blood flowed, covering his hands, slicking his grip. The smoke dissipated and still he stabbed, only stopping when the president no longer moved. He left the knife embedded as bullets peppered the hole. A flash of heat stroked his side. Without checking, Cain knew the bullet had gone clean through.

With one hard shove, Cain pushed Cambridge off the coffin and onto the dirt beside it. Then he disappeared on the opposite side, wedging himself between the casket and the dirt wall. Fire lanced his ribs. He glanced down at the wound then, saw where the blood darkened his shirt from hip to rib. With cold indifference, he pulled out his gun, and glanced out the hole.

"Get going!" Ian shouted as he dropped to the ground next to the grave. Breathing heavily, he reached down and grabbed Cain's forearm and pulled. Cain came up, his weapon firing. Bodies littered the ground. "They'll stay unconscious for at least ten minutes, but no more than twenty," Ian advised, before dropping his clip and jamming another into his pistol.

Vice President Bowden threw himself into the hole and covered the president with his body. Neither brother looked twice at the man.

"Lara's got Lassiter's men pinned from behind the building." Ian tossed Cain a spare pistol and watched him tuck it in his waistband. "I'll cover you from the front. Be careful," he warned. "Those bullets aren't real.

They're knockout pellets." Ian glanced at the roof as another shot exploded by his feet. "That friendly fire is from our minister," he spat sardonically, pointing to the top of the mausoleum. "I'm betting he's your man. One shot and I can take him down."

"No. Unconscious doesn't help me find Celeste."

"What's your plan?" Ian scanned the perimeter for Lara. She was crouched behind one of the larger grave markers a few yards away, systematically shooting the agents and troopers with the pellets.

"You distract Lassiter's men." Cain nodded toward the roof. "I'll do the rest."

Ian quirked his brow. "What's your backup plan?"

Cain's eyes met his brother's. "If I fail, make sure he does, too."

"My pleasure," Ian promised, his face set.

Cain took the mausoleum stairs in four long, strides. Gunfire whizzed past him as he hit the cement roof, rolled and palmed the smoke bombs. He squeezed each as he came up and whipped them at the deputies. Smoke exploded on the roof. Cain fired Ian's pistol taking down the remaining three men, but lost sight of Lassiter.

His wound burned and the blood-soaked shirt stuck to his skin, but Cain ignored both. From the opposite wall, Gabriel stepped forward, gun raised. "Like I said, Prometheus." He pointed his pistol toward Cain's wound. "The Pavenic woman has made you careless."

When he tries to kill us, he's going to do it in such a way that he'll show off his cunning.

Celeste's words collided with the truth of Gabriel's and fury darkened Cain's peripheral vision to a tempered black. In one fell swoop, all the emotion—anger, betrayal, guilt—he'd buried for the last three years poured out in a torrential storm and filled his head with a blinding red haze.

"Make it count, you son of a bitch, because I will." Cain threw his weapon away and advanced, his hands swinging loosely at his sides.

Eyes narrowed, Gabriel tightened his finger on the trigger, his aim focused on Cain's forehead.

The pistol discharged as Cain threw himself sideways. He felt the burn of the bullet's heat across his ear. Insane with rage, he lunged toward the killer, dodging the gun suddenly wedged between them. Its handle dug into his ribs, grinding cartilage. He hissed with pain, then smashed his forehead into Gabriel's face. The other man absorbed the hit with a grunt, but the shock loosened his hold. The gun flew from his fingers, over the wall, and clattered on the pavement below.

With his hands free, Cain tackled Gabriel but the other man was ready. He met Cain halfway. Their bodies slammed shoulder to shoulder. Cain's back teeth knocked together and he tasted blood. He grabbed Gabriel by the neck and squeezed. "Tell me where she is or I'll kill you now."

Gabriel's hands locked on Cain's wrists, but he didn't make any attempt to free himself. "Kill me and you kill the woman. Let me go and she still has a chance."

"A chance in hell." Cain hit Gabriel, enjoying the crunch of nose cartilage beneath his knuckles.

Cain saw Gabriel's gaze focus behind him. Cain swung him around, a split second before the blast of

Sheriff Lassiter's rifle. Gabriel stiffened, throwing both men off balance. Cain shifted, trying to break free but Gabriel hung on. Cain caught the surprise in Gabriel's eyes, even as the other man struggled to regain his balance. Unable to, the killer stumbled into the ledge. His calves smacked the brick, tripping him backward over the edge. Taking Cain with him.

"No!" Gabriel screamed as Cain made a frantic grab, his fingers catching only wisps of icy air. Doggedly, Cain struggled to keep his hold on the man as they both dropped.

Their bodies hit hard against iron. Cain felt the sickening thud, heard the crack of bone before he slammed against Gabriel, then dropped to the ground—alone.

Fire burned Cain's chest and he struggled to suck air into his lungs. His eyes locked on to Gabriel. The other man lay face up, impaled on the wrought-iron fence surrounding the Cambridge graves. Several spikes, now crimson with blood, pierced him mid-abdomen. His body hung across the top rail about four feet above the ground—like a broken puppet.

Cain scrambled to his feet, cursing his throbbing side, swiping at the blood running into his eyes.

"Don't you die yet, you bastard."

Gabriel gasped. Desperate, Cain grabbed the man's head and shoulders, and lifted them, knowing he was only adding a few precious seconds to the man's worthless life.

Gabriel's eyes fluttered open. "You think you've won, Prometheus?" A death rattle vibrated in his throat with each grinding syllable. "She'll die before you can reach her." His body spasmed. Blood and spittle frothed from his mouth and nose, forming crimson streaks down his chin and across his cheeks. He struggled for oxygen.

"Tell me, damn you!" Cain shouted into his face, his chest heaving, the rage and helplessness consuming him.

A sadistic smile played at the edges of Gabriel's mouth. "Tick. Tock," he whispered with his last breath.

In seconds, Cain was surrounded. He immediately placed his hands on his head and dropped to his knees. Two agents shoved him to the ground, face-first in the snow-patched dirt.

Something stung his eyes, dirt, blood—tears. He blinked them away. Other agents and troopers staggered around, still under the influence of the pellets' sedative—while many more still were out cold on the ground.

A foot pressed into the base of his neck, jarring his injury. Cain gritted his teeth. "Damn it, save the president," he yelled.

Ian and Lara hit the ground beside him, each eating dirt. In three quick snaps, Lara, Ian and Cain were handcuffed.

"Bring Cambridge over here." Cain tried to rise and took an elbow in the kidney for the effort.

"That'd be funny if he wasn't dead, you son of a bitch," Lassiter retorted, blood dripping from his forehead. The sheriff gripped his hair, yanking his head back, then cold steel dug into Cain's cheek. "Give me one goddamn reason you shouldn't join him," Lassiter asked, pressing the gun barrel hard enough for Cain to taste blood.

Ian swore. "Was she worth it, Cain? Enough to kill the president?" The betrayal was there, cemented in his brother's face. "Protect Cambridge and not harm anyone. That was the plan. That's why we used the smoking walls, the knock-out pellets." Ian jerked his head toward the dead man hanging on the fence. "Even Gabriel wasn't to die. Was this your backup plan?" Leveraging his chest off the ground, he twisted around to face Cain fully. "If Lara is brought down in this—"

"Shut up," the first Secret Service agent yelled and slammed the butt of a rifle across the back of Ian's head, knocking him back to the ground. "Or so help me, I'll—"

Lara hissed. Cain caught the flicker of concern in her green eyes before they flared. She struck out with her heel and nailed the agent in the kneecap. The man collapsed, howling.

The other raised his weapon, his intent clear. Ian rolled, caught the agent's leg with his ankles and yanked. The man hit the ground, his gun discharging into the air.

"Release them. Now!"

Chapter Seventeen

"I said release them!" President Cambridge stepped from the crowd of drugged troopers and agents. He grabbed Lassiter's arm, forcing the sheriff to let go of Cain. "Let them up! We don't have time for this!"

Blood dripped from the president's lip. His normally well-groomed hair stood in unnatural disarray. Instantly surrounded by protective bodies, the president shoved. "Get out of my way, you bloody idiots." Robert Cambridge grabbed his forehead and pulled. Prosthetic skin broke away from his face, revealing the stern expression of a younger man beneath.

The baritone voice was replaced by a clipped British accent. "You're one lucky bugger, Cain. If it had been Her Majesty's guards, your head would be lying next to your bloody ass by now."

"Damn it, Jordan, you took long enough." Cain raised his wrists behind his back. "Get these off," he ordered, urgency stressed every syllable.

"You heard the man. Unlock him," Jordan Beck demanded, wiping his bloody lip with the back of his

hand. His eyes narrowed, looking for the calm, calculating Prometheus who once had existed in his friend.
"Your president is at the White House." He tossed a
phone to one of the agents but didn't wait for the real
president to verify. "Now! Take off all their handcuffs,"
Jordan snapped, while Cain, finally free, grabbed his
confiscated gun from one of the troopers.

"I couldn't get out of the hole," Jordan complained.
"You nearly broke my bloody back, Yank, when you
tackled me." He undid his damaged shirt and threw the
concealed pad, filled with a thick red dye, to the ground.
"We got Bowden though. Nailed the bastard. When he
saw me move, he decided to try to stab me himself
while everyone was distracted. The ass didn't realize it
was a trick knife until it was too late. He won't be contracting any more hits."

Ian stepped toward one of the Secret Service men—
the one who had pistol-whipped him. He helped the
agent up before glancing at Lara. "Didn't think you
cared, Red."

"I don't," Lara snapped, shrugging off Ian's helping
hand. "I'm getting tired of being left in the dark, MacAlister," she continued, rounding on Cain, then shot a look
at Jordan. "Who the hell are you?"

"Jordan Beck," the Brit replied easily, picking off bits
of plastic and adhesive from his face.

"You're Jordan Beck?" Lara crossed her arms, taking
in the lanky body, the sharp British features.

"You've heard of me." Jordan grinned, then dropped
his voice. "Who else would MacAlister contact for this?
Roman convinced the president that he needed a decoy.

That's why the burial happened fast, and was kept so secretive. Even your father didn't know Cain had authorized the switch."

"Well, I'll be a—" Ian bit off his expletive.

Lassiter stepped forward and grabbed Cain's shirt. "You bastard!"

"You can have a piece of me later, Lassiter" Cain growled and yanked free. "Gabriel hid Celeste. She'll die if we don't find her soon." He'd been running Gabriel's last words through his mind. "Tick, tock. Tick, tock." His little voice kept nudging him. "Time's running out."

In the distance, shots ricocheted. Those who could, screamed warnings. Cain took off at a run, followed by the others.

It took only moments to reach the grave, but by then it was too late. Bowden had escaped. "Damn it," Cain roared. His eyes met Jordan's. "Go!"

Lassiter started running, directing those who were left to follow. Several agents and troopers had taken off through the woods, but none were capable of an aggressive pursuit.

Jordan shook his head, his features determined. "The way I figure, I owe Diana one, Yank. I'll get her."

"Her name's Celeste, damn it." Cain paused for only a moment, then looked at Ian. "Ian! You and Lara, go after Bowden."

Ian paused, "You need our help to find Celeste. Alone, you—"

"No. Do what I say!" Cain snapped, his fear palpable. "Nail the bastard, then come back and help me."

"Got it, boss."

"Tick tock." Jordan frowned as he watched Lara and Ian take off running. "A bomb?"

"Maybe," Cain bit out, not letting the fear take control. "He used one on her store."

"Too conventional," Jordan considered, his eyes narrowing on Cain's reactions. "Not clever enough."

"Clever?" Cain commented, then rushed back to Gabriel's body. Quickly, he searched his pockets, finding the coins in the coat. "Maine.

"The lighthouse," Cain yelled, shoving the quarters in his pocket, already running. "It operates with a clock mechanism."

THE GLOOM, chillingly eerie, darkened the interior of the tower, leaving only the lever in its limited light.

A queer calmness filled her. The weight, now little more than a foot above the nitroglycerin, told Celeste she had no choice. Her ankle no longer throbbed, nor did the raw wounds of her wrists burn.

Sweat drenched the T-shirt stuck to her back.

In the distance, beyond the walls of the tower, she heard the muffled burst of orders. Cain!

A sickness, dark and terror-filled, roiled within her belly, when she caught the fear that underlined his commands.

The noose tightened, biting into her neck, and she tried to still the trembling in her legs. Moments. They were only moments away.

She heard him brush against the door, heard his words through the pine. "Celeste, we're here, honey. Hold on!"

"No!" Celeste screamed, realizing even as she did that duct tape would stifle her warning.

And warning Cain would be useless.

Tears ran unchecked as she tightened her muscles. Her thoughts focused on the lever, and she shifted her hips, putting her feet in a front-kick position. She would only have one shot.

No regrets, she thought, her heart pounding. With her last thought of Cain, she launched forward.

Time slowed. In the back of her mind, she heard the crates crash, felt the rope tighten. Her foot hit the lever and the splintering snap of the wood ricocheted through her leg.

She swung back, self-preservation driving her to search for stability though she knew she wouldn't find it. The rope squeezed her throat, blocking what little air she had in her lungs.

Gabriel had sabotaged the lever.

She understood that in the split second that followed her kick.

Her lungs burned, her mouth parted, straining against the tape, unable to gasp. Through it all, she heard the clicking of the gears.

They both would die.

CAIN BRACED his foot against the door, levering to kick the pine in—when his little voice stopped him.

"Damn it!

"What?" Jordan came up from behind, and put his shoulder to the door, already primed to help.

"If I'm right, he'll use a bomb to kill her. Celeste said

he'll follow the same MO if he can." Cain ran his hand down the crevice of the door, searching for wires. "If that's the case this door will be rigged."

Cain glanced at Jordan. "Do you have your penlight?"

Jordan nodded, already reaching for his pocket. "You want to cut through?"

Cain snagged his own, then turned the thin dial at the base. "Set the length just past two inches. Any deeper we might cut through something other than the door."

Jordan copied his movements, then punched the black button.

The twin lasers sliced through the pine like butter. Within moments, Cain yanked the four-by-four square free and threw it to the ground then scrambled through the opening.

His heart lurched: Celeste was swinging in midair, her neck trapped in a noose.

Jordan raced to the mechanism brake, and spotted the broken lever. "Serious trouble," he gritted viciously.

"See how much time we've got," Cain yelled as he tossed his gun down—the laser already out and slicing the rope above Celeste's head.

"Celeste!" he shouted in her ear over the rush of his own pounding blood.

The rope parted and he slid the noose from her neck. When he pulled the tape from her mouth, she whimpered in pain as the adhesive tore skin from her lips.

"The bomb?" Her question came out raspy, sandpaper on sandpaper.

"We've got to get you out of here. Hold still," Cain said as he lasered through her cuffs.

"Coins." Celeste's throat was on fire, her jaw stiff. "We don't have time—"

"No." She shook her head, wincing as a thousand hot irons stabbed her neck. "Use…coins…in…gears."

Cain jerked his head, his eyes narrowing on the gearbox. "Jordan!" Hastily he set Celeste onto the ground and dug into his jeans pocket for the quarters from the cemetery.

Jordan was already there with his penlight laser, cutting the cover off. "Got it!"

Cain threw the quarters into the mechanism and slammed the lid shut. Time suspended for a moment as the coins rattled through. Suddenly a loud screech hit the air—the grinding of metal against metal—a high-pitched whine that threatened their eardrums.

Then silence. Sudden, deafening silence. The weight stopped, poised mere inches from the explosive.

Bracing himself, Cain lifted Celeste into his lap using the warmth of his body to give her strength. He smoothed away the sweaty tendrils of hair that clung to her forehead. He murmured unintelligible words against her cheek—rocked her back and forth.

"Now isn't this sweet?" Dan Bowden stood in the doorway, his eyes glinting with madness, his hand holding a 9mm Glock. "Can anyone join this party?"

Chapter Eighteen

The vice president nodded toward the bomb. The cruel twist of his mouth left his lips bloodless. "Looks like Gabriel's handiwork."

Cain froze, aware that his gun lay at least a foot away. And with Celeste in his lap, he wouldn't be able to move fast enough to reach it.

"I heard them, you know. Mercer and Olivia. She was concerned about her." He pointed his gun at Celeste but was talking to Cain, his breath coming in ragged bursts of air. "The old bat made the mistake of discussing it at a banquet when she thought no one was listening."

His teeth bared, Bowden yelled at Celeste. "You were supposed to be dead. You just couldn't leave it alone. You couldn't let Bobby Cambridge rest in peace!"

"She's dead now," Cain spat, but his eyes never wavered from Bowden. "She can't hear you." To prove his point he dropped her to the floor, praying she'd stay there. Then he stood, carefully placing himself between Bowden and Celeste.

"Don't move!" Bowden screamed, the shrill cry

came from somewhere amidst his madness. He waved his gun between Jordan and Cain while his other hand, out of habit, straightened the strand of hair from his forehead. Pushing it back. Pushing it back. In a steady continuous rhythm.

"Both of you will just have to listen for her," he insisted, spittle flying from his mouth, his pistol settling on Cain. "I've made deals, guarantees that would have put the United States back on the map. I would've gone down in history as the man who changed the world. But I couldn't do it walking in Cambridge's shadow." His laughed bitterly, but his eyes darted wildly, no longer settling. Watching for inner demons.

"You murdered a ten-year-old boy," Cain explained as fear clawed up his back with sharp talons. He beat it back down. "How does that make you a leader?"

Bowden sneered, his hand only stopping momentarily. "A necessary casualty. We are at war."

Cain heard Jordan inhale, knew the Brit was going to make a move. Cain's muscles tightened. "But the war isn't here." He gauged his chances and shifted a few inches toward his Glock.

"Of course it is. People must see it here to be impressed when I save them."

Celeste moaned and a cold sweat slicked Cain's skin.

"Look, Yank." Jordan's voice rose over another moan. "There's no need—" Jordan took a step forward, one hand raised, the other reaching for his gun.

"Don't!" Bowden fired his pistol. Jordan fell back, hit the wall and slid to the ground, leaving a stark trail of blood on the concrete behind.

"Damn it!" The Brit hissed with pain as his hand stifled the flow of blood at his shoulder. "What the hell happened to that ninety percent effective rate of this bloody material?"

"Don't worry," Bowden pointed his gun toward the nitroglycerin. "We're all going to die anyway—"

"No!" Cain barked, trying to draw Bowden's fire. He dove for Jordan's weapon, rolled and came to his knees, his finger compressing the trigger.

But he was too late.

The shot seemed to come from nowhere, but it caught Bowden right in the heart. He jerked once, dropping his gun, the dark eyes no longer glazed with insanity, only murky with confusion. Slowly, he crumpled onto the granite. Dead.

"No," Celeste whispered, Cain's pistol slipping from her fingers. "Not us, just you." Then her eyelids fluttered shut.

"THEY'RE going to be fine."

By the time the paramedics arrived, the firefighters had contained the nitro and Cain had gotten Celeste and Jordan out safely.

Celeste's wrists were bloody, the skin that wasn't torn already bruising. She'd fought hard to break free, fought hard to save Cain.

The handcuffs dangled from Cain's hand, while he watched the paramedics strap her to the stretcher. They'd made one attempt to treat Cain's injury, but the steel in his eyes drove them away.

Ian stood next to his brother, studying the play of emotion on Cain's features. "I like the change." He slapped Cain on the shoulder, but the tone of his voice softened. "It's nice to see you've got your soul back, big brother."

Celeste lay still, pale as death. Cain brushed her cheek, the only skin exposed. It had been so close. Too close.

Outside, while they waited for the helicopter to arrive, the paramedic had commented on the two things that had saved her life—the thick rope Gabriel had used and her petite frame. If not for those, she'd have broken her neck. As it was, she'd been only moments from unconsciousness and then strangulation.

It was too soon to tell if there'd be permanent damage to her vocal chords or scarring to her neck.

Yep, the paramedic had said, Miss Pavenic sure was lucky.

Cain disagreed. It was Celeste's strength that had saved her, not luck.

"Jordan?" Celeste rasped the question.

Cain pointed to the other stretcher where Jordan lay. "The bullet glanced off the collar bone. The hospital's going to keep him a few days, I'm sure, but it looks like he'll make it."

Celeste's eyes flickered. With relief, Cain eased over, placing his ear next to her lips. Her breath brushed against his cheek, tightening his gut, reminding him how close she'd come to dying.

"Cain."

He tucked a stray end of the blanket around her shoulder. "Don't talk, Gypsy, you could be damaging your voice."

She ignored the order. "Lighthouse…how?"

"Gabriel had the last set of quarters in his pocket. Maine. Once the president was dead, he would've left them for me, I'm sure."

Celeste's eyes fluttered closed on the tears starting to gather. "Why didn't you…tell me…about Mercer?"

"At the time, I wasn't sure he'd survive. It wasn't important to the mission."

"Like…Quamar…at warehouse?" Her voice, now grits of sandpaper, bit into him. "Like…Lassiter's…interrogation?"

Her tone was filled with more than pain from the injury, more than fatigue or sorrow. Underlying both, Cain heard accusation, defeat.

"I had my reasons, Celeste. Good reasons."

"No."

He should've welcomed the finality in her answer. He'd gotten his answers, his pound of flesh. That's what he'd wanted only the day before. Instead, bitterness rose up in him, savage and mean. In spite of it, he kept his voice gentle. "I did it to protect you, Gypsy. The more you became involved, the more chance—"

"I…protect…me," Celeste protested weakly. "You… me…" she rasped. "Never…us." She turned her head away, tears flowing unchecked. "Never…trust."

Vulnerability welled in him, unexpected, riding shotgun to his anger. "Damn it, this isn't the place—"

"No…done," she argued. "You…agreed…stay… away."

The loud whop of the helicopter could be heard in the distance. "Sir," one of the paramedics, a gray-haired man, his face lined with experience, insisted. His eyes were sympathetic but determined. "We need to take her up to the road."

"All right," Cain agreed, knowing it wasn't the time to settle things between them.

"Sir, you really need to get yourself treated." The paramedic pointed to Cain's side where dried blood kept the shirt sealed to the wound. "I can have someone take you to the nearest hospital."

Cain nodded to the man, not recognizing him from the fire the night before.

God, had it been that recent? It seemed as though a lifetime had passed, but it had taken them a little less than twenty-four hours to stop Gabriel.

Still, he couldn't stop the whispers of his little voice.

They'd won against Gabriel, but what had he lost in the process?

Chapter Nineteen

Everything was white outside. Not a stark, hurt-your-eyes kind of white, Celeste mused absently, but the soft-focus white that soothed and tempted most to be lazy. Just the kind of weather that made kids wish for a day off from school.

For the hundredth time that week, she forced the heartache away. After all, she thought stubbornly, how many people get to spend an evening visiting—

"Miss Pavenic?"

Startled, Celeste swung around from the window overlooking the snowy White House lawn.

"Miss Pavenic?" A female voice questioned again.

"Yes." Celeste cleared her throat, embarrassed still over its unnatural huskiness. A permanent reminder of her heroism, the specialist had said. "I'm sorry, I'm a little jet-lagged."

"I understand." The woman appeared to be in her mid-forties, a short, stylish brunette in an efficient dark burgundy business suit. In one hand she carried a day planner, with the other she gestured toward a long hall.

"I'm Martha Fisher. President Cambridge's personal assistant. The president is ready to see you now."

Celeste followed the older woman through a door into a narrow hall.

"I apologize for the delay. Our schedule is a little bit off this evening."

"I understand." Celeste smoothed a hand over the V-neck of her simple navy-blue suit, trying not to let her fingers touch her bandaged neck self-consciously.

Turned out Gabriel had been nothing more than an ex-mercenary named André Bovic. A man who'd advanced his career by refining his talents and education.

It had been two weeks since he had died. Two weeks of interviews, flash bulbs, crowds and the paparazzi's attention that had turned her into an overnight celebrity—something she didn't want, but suspected Jon Mercer had triggered.

Once Mercer's resurrection became public, the frenzy was unimaginable. After all, it wasn't every day the vice president was involved in a scandal. The media sensed blood, and, like piranhas after prey, they demanded details.

And they'd gotten them. The vice president had left detailed notes of his plot, maybe hoping one day to publish it. Bowden had revealed his desire for an almost Hitleresque world. In order to have it, he needed to guarantee his place as president. He'd contracted the hits and planted Bremer's phone number on Celeste's cell.

Saddened, Celeste thought of all those people dead because of his madness. Bobby, Grams, Olivia Cambridge, the prostitute Joyce Raines. Bowden had manipulated the phone records, forged documents, provided

Gabriel with Cain's file and details of Mercer's injuries that the president had entrusted him with.

The felony counts were endless.

As was the media's interest.

Celeste's legs wobbled only a bit as she followed Ms. Fisher down the last of the wide halls.

Martha Fisher held open a door and Celeste stepped into the Oval Office.

Robert Cambridge turned from the large windows overlooking the famous Rose Garden and crossed the deep, navy-blue rug emblazoned with the Presidential Seal. A flutter swept through Celeste's stomach. She couldn't believe she was actually standing here, alone, with the President of the United States.

And he wasn't having her arrested.

"Miss Pavenic." He grasped her hand, his smile warm and reassuring. She noticed he'd taken off his suit jacket, loosened his tastefully patriotic red-and-blue pinstriped tie and rolled up the cuffs of his white Armani shirt. The casualness could've come from a long presidential day, but she figured that more than likely he'd dressed down to put her at ease.

"I want to thank you for coming today." His eyes, a soft leather-brown, shadowed with remorse when they touched first on her neck then on the bandages around her wrists. "Frankly, I wasn't sure if you would."

"I have to admit, I was surprised." Celeste smiled and discreetly—because of a sharp twinge of pain—tugged her hand free. The lacerations, although deep, were healing quickly, along with her neck bruises, which had faded to a dull yellow.

"Please, so we can talk." He indicated a plush cream couch to her right. Instead of taking the opposite couch though, he sat next to her, surprising her. "First of all, I want to apologize for my actions and conduct after Bobby's death. You did your best, just as I did, in trying to protect him. But I couldn't see that at the time."

"Understandably. You were set up just as much as I was." Slowly, Celeste sorted through her words. "More so because of your emotional state at the time. I believe the worst thing that can happen to parents is the loss of a child." It emptied the soul of the family, leaving their spirits whisper-thin. Bobby's murder would be an experience that would haunt her for the rest of her life. "And to be honest, Mr. President, you couldn't have blamed me any more than I blamed myself."

"I'm sorry for that, too," he said gently and cleared his throat. Instantly changing the mood, he smiled. Not the politician's smile she'd seen plastered across the papers but a genuinely kind smile. "I haven't thanked you properly for saving my life."

"It really isn't necessary—"

"But it is. If I had my way, you'd receive a medal. And you still may." He patted her shoulder. "But for now, I want to thank you personally." He leaned over until his lips lightly brushed her cheek. "Thank you."

Startled, Celeste stared at him until he winked. A smile tugged at her lips. "You're welcome."

"Now…" He settled back into the cushion and studied her for a moment, his solemn expression reminding her more of a father's than of a world leader's. "…I have an official favor to ask."

Celeste waited, felt the hum of nervousness between her shoulder blades.

"I want you to work for us again. Work for Labyrinth."

A month ago, Celeste would never have considered it. But a month ago, she'd believed herself a failure.

"You are under no obligation, of course." The president cleared his throat. "But I'd like to point out that with no store and a only a hotel for your current home, your future—"

"I accept."

It was President Cambridge's turn to be startled. "You do?"

"Oh, yes." She laughed slightly, understanding his surprise. It was no greater than her own. "But I do have one concern." All humor disappeared. "I've achieved some notoriety because of the events in Shadow Point."

"Your notoriety, in this case, will help us. For now, your speaking schedule can be adapted to wherever we need you. You've proven quite effective in the field. Later, we're hoping to utilize your talents in our recruiting process." He patted her hand. "Hold on one moment." In two quick strides, he reached his desk and hit the intercom. "Ms. Fisher?"

"Yes, Mr. President."

"Could you please catch my prior appointment? I need him to join Ms. Pavenic and myself for a moment."

"Yes, Mr. President. He's still here."

Celeste quirked a brow in question just as the door opened behind her. Apprehension skittered up her spine. She twisted around.

Cain.

He crossed the room with his usual predatory grace, dressed in his customary black snug-fitting slacks, tie and shirt. Leaner, with sharper edges, Cain studied her. His jaw, she noted, was shadowed with dark whiskers. If she'd thought he looked lethal before, it didn't compare to now.

"Mr. President." He shook hands with Cambridge. The greeting was casual, almost too casual, Celeste realized and squared her shoulders.

"Cain." The president nodded toward Celeste. "Miss Pavenic has agreed to rejoin Labyrinth."

"Good." Cain replied evenly, his features impassive.

Celeste's mouth tightened, understanding. "You've taken over as director."

"Jon decided to retire earlier than expected." Cambridge's answer did nothing to disperse the growing tension in the air. "And although it hasn't been made public yet, he has graciously accepted my appointment as vice president. Of course, both Houses need to agree. But considering his record, there shouldn't be any problem."

"You'll be working for me, Celeste," Cain emphasized.

Under duress, she was sure.

"Your field duties will be limited, of course."

"Is that right?" Irritated that Cain was still protecting her, Celeste turned to Cambridge. "I've reconsidered, Mr. President. And although I'm flattered, I'm declining your offer."

"Why?" Cain's question was bland, almost bored. She understood the thinly veiled warning for what it was. He wasn't going to back down.

"Because I have that right." She scowled, her fist

tightening on the strap of her leather purse. She tried to calm herself with a deep breath.

"Of course you do." The president hesitated, obviously puzzled. "But I was hoping—"

Cain grasped her arm and started toward the door. "I know you're a busy man, Mr. President. So we'll take our...negotiations...elsewhere."

"No, we won't." Her mouth firmed, her heels dug in. "Since the president offered me the job, I expect to deal with him and only him."

"Yes, well..." Robert Cambridge moved to the door, his brows furrowed with curiosity. "Actually, Cain requested your reinstatement. I merely lent my support. So you do need to discuss your concerns with him, Miss Pavenic." His gaze moved warmly over Celeste. "Thank you again for all you've done for my family."

"Thank you, sir." Realizing she'd lost her only ally, Celeste turned on Cain. "Unfortunately, I'm running late for another meeting. I'll contact your office so we can set up an appointment."

"No," Cain drawled.

Before Celeste could react, he picked her up and swung her over his shoulder like a sack of potatoes. Careful to avoid her injuries, he walked through the door.

Cambridge's stifled laughter followed them.

Chapter Twenty

Celeste arched her back, hoping to elicit some help, but no one from the offices along the corridor moved, although several men and women stared. Her cheeks flushed with embarrassment, feeding her fury. Apparently, not even the Secret Service challenged Cain MacAlister. "Are you crazy? What are you doing?" she hissed.

"If I've learned nothing else in the past few weeks, I've learned you don't understand the word *stay*." He re-adjusted his arm, pinning her skirt to the back of her knees. "And frankly, you could drive any man insane."

Cain reached the elevator and jabbed the button. "I'm taking you somewhere private, so we can talk about the future."

"Put me down!" Longing pulled at her, hard and deep, igniting a flare of irritation. She punched his backside, almost hurting her knuckles on the tight, firm muscles.

"No." The elevator doors slid closed, and Celeste buried her face against his back. He smelled of leather and soap. Her fists curled against the temptation to in-hale more deeply.

"Why, Cain?" She gritted her teeth in frustration. Frustration not from being carried through the White House in such a humiliating manner, but from fear of letting her feelings for him show. "Why did you come here? Ms. Fisher didn't just *catch* you. You were waiting." They hadn't fooled her, and she wanted him to know it.

"The pretense was the president's idea." His voice, husky with patience, vibrated across her thighs. Desire shot through her, causing a sharp intake of air.

Outside, a limo was waiting. Celeste only caught a glimpse of it before he slid her down the front of him, causing a jolt when thigh touched hip. "He wanted the chance to thank you personally for what you did," Cain continued casually, as if his carrying a woman through the White House was an everyday occurrence. "And to find out if you'd forgiven him."

Before she could reply, the limousine driver swung open the door, and caught Celeste's eye. "Jordan!"

"At your service, Poppet." Relieved to find another ally, Celeste couldn't help but smile over the nickname he'd given her. For the last two weeks, Jordan Beck had made it his business to become her friend. He'd confessed to being the reason Cain hadn't been with her during Bobby's kidnapping and the aftermath. When Celeste admitted that she'd already come to terms with Cain's decision, knowing it couldn't have happened any other way, Jordan seemed relieved.

"I'm so glad to see you," she told Jordan, returning his quick hug, careful not to jar the sling that held his arm.

Dressed in a leather jacket and jeans, Jordan Beck looked nothing like a chauffeur. "Actually, I insisted on driving. I thought you needed someone to cover that lovely tush for a bit, and I wanted to make sure this bloke here didn't intimidate you."

For the sake of time, Cain let the comment pass. "All right, Beck. You've said your hellos." Capturing Celeste's elbow, Cain urged her inside the car, not surprised when she refused to move.

He sighed, letting his impatience show. He wanted her in the car and in his arms. So much so, he didn't care if Jordan heard. "I've waited long enough to talk to you, Celeste. You wouldn't see me at the hospital, wouldn't return my calls at the hotel. If I have to pick you up and toss you in, I will."

Uncertainty had her biting her lip, and Cain pushed his advantage. When she slid a glance at Jordan, Cain's glare followed.

Jordan shrugged, but a grin tugged at his mouth. "It's the least you could do, Poppet. The man has been chomping at the bit all week."

"Jordan—" Cain warned, biting off the rest of his remark and instead turned back to Celeste. "Get in."

Lifting her chin, she stepped into the limo. "Raise the privacy window, Beck. You know where we're headed." Cain eased onto the leather upholstery after a quick salute from his friend. Celeste sat as far away from him as possible. Which, considering it was a stretch limo, was quite a few feet. His mouth twisted wryly over the distance. "Just in case we decide to neck."

The slight widening of Celeste's eyes, and the subtle flush to her cheeks pleased him and he poured himself two fingers of whiskey. MacAlister whiskey. A present from his father. Cain lifted the glass, asking, and she shook her head.

"Just where are we headed?"

Deliberately misunderstanding, Cain said. "That's what I want to find out." He drank the whiskey, then set the glass aside.

"You never used to play games, Cain," she whispered.

Wanting to skip the words, but knowing the explanations needed to come first, he leaned forward and placed his forearms on his knees. "Remember when you said we all have our pasts to deal with? Well, you were right, we all do. Mercer, Quamar. You. Myself."

Her jaw flexed but she didn't look Cain's way. Instead she continued to gaze through the window as Washington, D.C., passed by. "How is Quamar?"

"He came out of the coma a few days ago." Cain's hesitation brought her around.

"But," she prompted.

"He's blind, Celeste." Cain had visited Quamar the day before. The giant seemed in good spirits, but Cain had recognized his friend's underlying fear. "He's undergoing a battery of tests and his doctors are considering surgery. The prognosis is good."

"Is he allowed visitors?"

"Yes." He reached over to touch her arm, but she shifted away. "Damn it." He yanked a hand through his hair. It was either that or yank her into his lap.

"Remember when you accused me of being the self-appointed protector of mankind? You were right." He braced his elbows on his knees, and locked his hands together. "Prometheus was the god who provided man with fire against Zeus's wishes. So, in retaliation, Zeus had him chained to a rock where a giant eagle tore at his liver all day, only to have it grow back every night for the eagle to devour again."

"I know the story."

"Part of me *is* Prometheus. And I wouldn't change that. Because that's what kept me alive."

"If we agree—"

Cain wasn't finished. "But you're Lachesis, too, Celeste. And Diana. No matter how much you run away, they remain a part of you. That's why the Labyrinth job is yours. Not to prove anything to you, but because I know you'll do a damned good job."

"It's mine with restrictions," she corrected, not bothering to hide her bitterness.

"That's right. Not to protect you, but to train you. I wouldn't send any operative out in the field without proper training. Especially not one I'm in love with."

A small flame of hope flared, but she brushed it away. "Loving me is not enough. Not anymore. I'm not sure it ever was." Celeste swung away, unable to deal with the hurt that squeezed her chest. "I thought that the more I cared for you, the more I'd understand you. But the reality is that the more you care for me, the more barriers you put up preventing me from seeing into you. Even when we're…" She stopped unable to continue.

"Making love?" he murmured rhetorically. "Not any more. No more secrets—unless I'm held to the restrictions by my job."

"Why should I believe you?"

"You think I'm lying? This thing between us—you

think that's a lie, too?" Through his fury, he recognized the truth. Why should she believe him? Up to this moment, the only time he'd shared any part of himself with her was when he'd whispered it as she lay half-unconscious in the lighthouse.

Celeste stared at him, confusion rimming the deep blue of her eyes, furrowing her brow. A strange tenderness swept through Cain, dissipating the anger, the frustration.

He almost gave in to the urge to touch her, the ache to hold her. But unless she came willingly, the gesture was hollow. "Fate bonded us. Maybe I'd been so lost in a dark, emotionless hole that I needed someone like you, something like this to bring me out of it."

He joined her on her seat, craving her nearness, wanting to comfort her. "Gabriel's dead. He wouldn't be if you hadn't done your job. I…" He gave in then and tipped her chin up. "…would be dead, if you hadn't."

He brought his face close, until they were nose to nose. "You made the call, Celeste." Anger flashed across his feature, startling her.

For the first time she noticed. All his emotions—love, hurt, rage—were there on his face, something the old Cain would never have allowed, would never have shared.

Anger, frustration, desperation gushed through her. She fought them off. And the tears. The tears were the hardest. "I don't know what you want from me, but whatever it is, I can't give it to you."

"I just want your love. And your trust—when I've earned it again. Nothing else. I had to fight through hell and back to get to the feelings I have. And like Prometheus, I've had my insides eaten out again and again."

His forehead tipped against hers. His breath came in shaky heaves. He was frightened. Just as she was. Through her mind flashed an image of a two-story house, kids running through a sprinkler screaming, a puppy nipping at their ankles.

"You once told me you loved me, Celeste. I won't let you take it back, because only you can save me."

"No," she whispered, but she felt the wall around her heart splinter, each shard driving deep. Her jaw trembled, and she clenched it. "It's not that easy. Finally, in the past few weeks, I'm beginning to realize who I am. What I am. I'm strong. Not invincible, but strong. All my life I leaned on Grams, Jon, even you— using what others thought of me to fill the empty void inside me. I don't need that anymore. I don't need you or anyone anymore, for that matter. I can rely on myself, take care of myself, Cain. I might love you, but I don't need your love back. I'll survive better without it."

"Do you hear yourself?" he growled, his gaze pinning her to her seat. "You can survive by yourself and take care of yourself. You don't need love or emotion or anyone in order to live the life you've chosen?" Desperation laced each syllable he uttered. He shifted away, almost as if he couldn't bear the closeness any longer.

The car slowed to a stop and the privacy window lowered, the hum of it doing nothing to dissipate the tension. "Cain."

Cain scowled, the bite in his words showing his displeasure over the interruption. "What is it, Jordan?"

"Our guest is getting restless up here. He's starting

to take his irritation out on the passenger seat. I thought I might toss him back with you for a while."

A sharp yowl hit the walls of the limo. Celeste glanced over as Jordan, one-handed, dropped Pan through the window onto the bench seat below. An emerald-green bow puffed up behind the back of his head, but it wasn't until Pan sauntered forward that she saw the sapphire ring hanging from his collar. Her eyes widened, but she didn't acknowledge it, didn't want to think about its meaning. "Where did you come from?"

"Your hotel." Cain uncoiled from beside Celeste, then leaned over and picked Pan up. "I snagged him from your room along with your luggage."

"Why?"

"Because I thought you and your family would like to spend some time with my family before you started work." Cain's scowl darkened; his response was surly and impatient.

"I think I'll pass, Cain. There's no need to prolong—"

"What about Pan?" He handed the cat to Celeste. "Do you still need him?"

"Of course." She stroked the minklike coat, hearing the purr of pleasure, ignoring the ring clinking against his collar. "He's my responsibility." Her hand froze, realizing.

"Your responsibility?" Startled, she caught the stab of anger in his question, the accusation. "Only two weeks ago, you would have said he was your family."

"He is." She gathered Pan close to her chest, burying her trembling fingers in his fur. "I love Pan. You know that."

Cain wouldn't let her off that easily. Couldn't. There was too much at stake for both of them. He rubbed his eyes. "Don't become what you hated, Celeste. Don't become me—or at least what I used to be."

"You did what you had to do. Duty means you make sacrifices." Celeste put Pan onto the floor.

"That's the excuse I used." He took her hand, humbled when she unconsciously gripped it back. "Three years ago, I deliberately seduced you. I didn't care about you or what you wanted. I'd wanted the serenity you brought to my life and made sure I left you with no other choice."

"I wanted to be seduced," she admitted quietly, but it was the underlying shame that caught like a hook in his heart. "You didn't do anything I hadn't wished for."

"But you also wanted more. At the time, I knew I couldn't give it to you. But I can now," Cain rasped, his voice raw with what he'd lost. He brushed away a tendril of hair from her cheek. "I've never begged anyone. But I'm begging you now."

His words pierced Celeste like tiny, sharp arrows, bringing down the last of the barriers that constricted her heart. She searched deep into the pewter of Cain's eyes, now tinted with regret.

"I'm sorry, Celeste. Forgive me." His hand slipped over her heart, his forehead tipped against hers. "I love you. I loved you the first moment we met, I've loved you with every breath I've taken since."

He used his thumb to brush away a tear on her cheek. "I can't promise a life of bliss," he whispered. His hand curved around the back of her neck, tilting her head back. "But I do know that without you, I'm only half alive."

Her hand caressed his jaw, her fingers traced the hard lines of his features—knowing that the power that lay just beneath the surface would not make their life easy.

Celeste realized that she wanted the flesh-and-blood man before her—and the exciting roller coaster of emotions that came with him. A small smile tilted her lips. "Partners?"

He groaned, trembling as his hand gripped hers. "Partners." He lifted her onto his lap. Automatically, her legs locked around him as his mouth found hers, this time with a need she felt confident she could fill. And she gave herself freely. Because Cain had saved her too.

"I'm going to work for Labyrinth," she said against his lips, and happiness flowed through her, sweet and warm.

"I'm going to be your boss," he reminded her, determined.

"That's okay." She nipped his jaw, finally feeling complete, whole. "Because someday I plan to be *your* boss."

"What makes you think so?" he teased, while his hands danced up her spine, making her squirm, making the heat between them flare.

"If I'm tough enough to love you…" She tugged his hair to make him stop, but instead her fingers caressed its silky texture. "…then I certainly have the guts to boss you around."

He nuzzled her neck, laughing, and the rumbling sent shivers quaking through her limbs. She'd done that, she thought. She'd made him happy.

"I do love you, Cain."

With a groan, his hand caught hers, warm and welcoming. Slowly, he slid her body back onto the seat then

knelt before her. Ignoring a high-pitched yowl from
Pan, he tugged the green ribbon and the solitaire ring
free from the cat's neck.

"Cain?"

"Celeste?" Cain mimicked her softly, then held out
the ring. Blue fire flashed beneath the limo's interior
lights. "I know this might be too soon, but I can't wait."
Cain's mouth tilted, sexy, teasing—taking her breath
away. "I guess impatience has become one of my newly
discovered traits."

"Could work for me." Her lips curved in a secret
feminine smile as he slipped the sapphire band on her
finger.

"I didn't think I had anything—not even you," she
said, not bothering to hide the tears that welled in her
eyes. "Now I don't want anything but you." Cain gathered her close, and she felt the tension drain from his
body. She shivered as his breath fanned her skin. Tipping
her head to one side, she allowed him more access.

Cain leaned back, taking her with him until she
sprawled over him, limbs entwined. His hand slid up her
thigh, groaning when he touched a spot of bare skin
above the silken hose. "White cotton?" he asked rhetorically, passion turning his eyes sleek silver.

"Always."

Gently, almost reverently, he kissed the side of her
mouth. "I love you," he murmured, linking her hands
behind her back, drawing her tight. Desire tripped
through her and she melted into him.

"You pick the damnedest times to go soft on me,
Gypsy."

"And no bed in sight." She laughed wickedly, letting her love filter through.

His fist hit a button on the nearby bar. Suddenly the lounging seat on the other side of the limo flipped, and the backrest slid down, revealing a full-size bed.

He caught her earlobe tenderly between his teeth. Goose bumps chased down her neck. "You were saying?"

Pan jumped onto the bed and looked at Celeste, his eyes hooded and lazy. With a languid yawn, he circled twice and settled down with a flick of his tail. Celeste glanced from the cat to the bed to her man. With tender fingers, she cupped his cheek and lowered her lips to his.

"Stay."

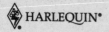
HARLEQUIN®

INTRIGUE

PRESENTS

ROCKY MOUNTAIN SAFEHOUSE

a miniseries featuring

UNDERCOVER COLORADO
On sale March 2006

and

MURDER ON THE MOUNTAIN
On sale April 2006

BY CASSIE MILES

Nestled in the Colorado Rockies, this safe house protects the nation's finest—from undercover operatives to politicians hiding from assassins. As deadly elements find their way to this haven, a select few can keep the inhabitants from facing the ultimate danger....

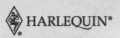

HARLEQUIN®

INTRIGUE®

COMING NEXT MONTH

#909 INVESTIGATING 101 by Debra Webb
Colby Agency: New Recruits
New recruit Todd Thompson skips basic training and jumps right into danger when he helps researcher Serena Blake investigate a horrifying case involving stolen identities and missing children.

#910 MURDER ON THE MOUNTAIN by Cassie Miles
Rocky Mountain Safe House
While hosting Homeland Security exercises at her lodge-turned-safe house, FBI agent Julia Last discovers the body of a five-star general in a locked room. And when a sudden blizzard traps her and the local deputy sheriff in with the murderer, will they become the next victims?

#911 AT CLOSE RANGE by Jessica Andersen
Bear Claw Creek Crime Lab
Can rival CSIs Seth Varitek and Cassie Dumont set aside their differences to take down a serial killer who has returned west and trapped them within close proximity?

#912 THE SECRET NIGHT by Rebecca York
43 Light Street
Every lover Nicholas Vickers takes, he eventually loses forever. But when a young woman pleads for his help on his doorstep, he can't refuse. But can he resist her before his horrible secret dooms them both?

#913 UNEXPECTED FATHER by Delores Fossen
Lilly Nelson awakens from a coma to find she's given birth to a daughter she didn't even know she conceived. But when she finds her baby in the protective care of a tough-as-nails Texas cop, Lilly will do anything to make up for lost time, including tracking down the people who put her in the coma in the first place.

#914 WHEN A STRANGER CALLS by Kathleen Long
Camille Tarlington tried to bury the senseless tragedy of her past, but when a young lawyer with a shared secret presents her with new evidence, she's forced to reconsider everything she ever held true.